MW01138946

Letters to Kezia

Book Two of the Puritan Chronicles

PENI JO RENNER

ISBN: 978-1-4834-6088-8 (sc)
ISBN: 978-1-4834-6087-1 (e)

Lulu Publishing Services rev. date: 11/21/2016

In the tradition of author Peni Jo Renner's gripping debut novel, *Puritan Witch: The Redemption of Rebecca Eames*, *Letters to Kezia* recounts the tale of courageous, compassionate, and relatable Mary, whose connection to Rebecca and her family is unforeseen and profound. The reader is captivated at the very first page, as *Letters to Kezia* is a story of forbidden love, deep family secrets, intrigue, murder, and atonement. Another beautifully written triumph for this author, whose immense gift for story-telling transports the reader into each scene so deftly, one can almost smell the wood smoke and hear the crackling of the fire in the hearth.

-- Kelly Z. Conrad, award-winning author of *Shaman*

Peni Jo Renner enthralled readers with *Puritan Witch*, the ordeal of Rebecca Eames, who was condemned to hang from Salem's gallows as a witch. Now the Eames saga continues as Peni uses her special brand of witchery to bring Mary Case and Daniel Eames to vivid life, and shows us just how much a young woman will risk for love. *Letters to Kezia* is a poignant, true-life tale from colonial New England's heartland which will captivate you, and keep you guessing until the end.

—Jo Ann Butler, author of *Rebel Puritan*
and *The Reputed Wife*

After the publication of *Puritan Witch,* I came in contact
with a multitude of distant cousins who are also descendants
of Rebecca Blake Eames. This book is dedicated to all those
cousins I've come to know, and to those I've yet to meet.
And especially for Dave.
Y.A.M.V.H.

The author is especially grateful to Carol Majahad, Executive Director of the North Andover Historical Society in North Andover, Massachussets. Thanks again, Carol, for all your fact-checking and support!

Chapter One

September, 1712
Hereford, CT

"Mother, what are these papers? I found them at the bottom of the trunk whilst fetching the quilts."

Mary Case glanced up from her sewing as she bit off the thread. Her eighteen-year-old daughter Kezia stood before her. The girl's green eyes, so like her father's, glittered with curiosity. It was a pleasant September morning and Mary had just enough time to finish hemming a neighbor's skirt before her husband, Kezia's stepfather, returned home for supper. Alarm blanched her already-pallid face even before she saw the bundle of sealed parchment in her daughter's long-fingered hand.

"Are they letters?" the young woman pressed. "My name is on it above the seal--"

The skirt fell from Mary's lap as she rose from the large rock she'd been sitting on. Even as she reached out for the papers, Kezia pressed them to her chest possessively. "It's about who my real father is, isn't it?" the girl speculated, color draining from her own pretty face.

Mary's eyes left Kezia's and regarded the packet of letters with trepidation. She sank back onto the large rock. *Shall I allow her to read them?* She pressed her sweaty palms against the cool grey limestone, willing it to give her an answer. For years, she found solace whenever she was near the boulder. Mimicking the grey of Mary's eyes, it was as big as a ram and looked like an oversized loaf of bread rising amidst the copse of poplar trees. When the weather allowed, it was her favorite place to sew. But now the rock refused to offer any comfort. She felt defeated and swallowed over the thickness that grew in her throat.

"I hoped you wouldn't come across them 'til I gave up the ghost," she confessed in a small voice. "But you are of age, and you have a right to know your parentage….."

"So may I read them now?" Kezia asked, her voice cracking nervously.

A soft breeze sent a yellow leaf skittering across the rock before it tumbled to the ground to land onto Mary's linen-covered sewing basket. Mary sighed. *So be it.* She met her daughter's anxious face and said, "Aye. Read them now, but not in my presence." She retrieved the fallen skirt and grasped the handle of her sewing basket. "I've got to deliver this skirt to Goody Drake. Mind the pot on the hearth .The beans should be done simmering by the time your stepfather returns home."

"Will Father be home before sundown?"

"I suspect he will."

Mary's overbite sank into her bottom lip, her heart blooming with fierce pride at the lovely woman her daughter had grown into. Tall and slender with her father's red hair, Kezia had been nothing but a blessing. Teased for being baseborn, Kezia handled her peers' taunts with aplomb not often seen in children. Kezia had always known Mary's husband was not her natural father, but that didn't prevent a loving bond from forming between them.

Hot tears warmed the back of Mary's eyes as a lump formed in her throat. Without another word, she turned to leave, glancing back only once. Kezia was seated on the sun-dappled rock, her head bent as she broke the seal on the packet of parchment. The almost imperceptible sound of the wax breaking made Mary gasp nervously.

Forgive me, my darling girl. Don't judge us too harshly, your father and I, she wanted to say. She again bit her bottom lip to keep from crying, and spun away so quickly the yellow leaf fluttered from the basket and landed on the ground, unnoticed.

After her mother left, Kezia opened the packet of parchment with reverence. She unfolded the papers slowly, revealing her mother's delicate scrawl. Her mother had written over someone else's handwriting, making it difficult to read. Apparently Mary had written over a minister's penned sermon notes. Taking a deep breath, Kezia began to read:

> *My darling Kezia,*
>
> *It is with a broken and forlorn heart that I put quill and ink to this parchment on this seventh day of November, in the year 1695.*
>
> *Providence has never smiled upon me, and two summers ago it sent such an ill fate my way I saw no means to avoid it.*
>
> *After Mother died, Father took the position as pastor in Hereford. It was only he and I left to tend to Lizzie. My little sister was only in her ninth year, and afflicted with the falling sickness. I, being a spinster of twenty years, took it upon myself to rear my sister in Mother's absence.*
>
> *We lived in the rectory next to the meeting house. The new minister and his dutiful daughters were welcomed warmly enough, but I never felt truly accepted, due to my peculiar grey eyes and overlapping front teeth. As for sweet Lizzie, her peers treated her most cruelly.*
>
> *My fall, as great as that of Adam and Eve in the Garden, began on a Lecture Day in August. Father's deep baritone held his audience spellbound as he and his assistant minister, Noah Parker, stood in the church yard with several magistrates near them, their expressions doleful as the branding iron with the T on the end glowed red in the small fire pit. Smoke rose in a straight column, obscuring the face of the thief who stood with his head and hands locked in the pillory. He'd been caught in the very act of ransacking Goody Ellis' larder. Her grown son, Thomas, had apprehended him, and bound him in their barn until Constable Hart collected him. Now the guilty man stood*

bent with his head and hands locked in the pillory, one of three hideous contraptions for punishment. The stocks and the whipping post stood empty nearby as if jealous of the pillory for its victim.

I stood amidst my peers, a basket containing linen strips and a pot of ointment at my feet. Lizzie stood before me, mindlessly chewing her coif strings. For the second time that afternoon, I plucked them from her mouth, soggy with saliva. It was a nervous habit of hers, and I knew before Father's lecture was over, the strings would again disappear behind Lizzie's plump lips.

Noah Parker stood off to the side, stark white scarf falling around his neck. Beneath his tall-crowned hat, his small facial features clustered together tightly in a square, doughy face. For reasons unclear to me at the time, both Father and Noah seemed to have agreed that Noah and I would one day wed. Neither of us displayed any genuine interest in each other, but being the dutiful minister's daughter, I resigned myself to my fate.

That day I kept my gaze on Lizzie's coifed head, my hands resting on her shoulders. I hoped the impending agony the thief was about to endure would not send her into one of her fits. For that reason, I always kept two physicks in my velvet waist pouch. One contained tincture of motherwort to quiet her fits; the other was a pot of hartshorn to rouse her should she faint.

Late August, 1693
Hereford, Connecticut

"And so it is, with righteous authority, we brand this stranger a thief, so that all may know of his crime."

After Reverend Case spoke those words, Constable Absalom Hart lumbered forward. An impressively large man, his presence would be intimidating if it weren't the sad gentleness in his brown eyes. To Mary, he gave the impression of an overgrown bear cub who had no inkling of his own physical strength. She watched as Hart plucked the glowing branding iron from the coals. His somber face registered reluctance as he held the iron in his large hands. Hart glanced at his young deputy, James for a moment as if in hesitation. Mary felt Lizzie squirm and press her face into her skirts. Rubbing her sister's small back, she stood mesmerized by the appearance of the pilloried man.

Filthy red curls flowed from beneath his worn felt hat. Beneath the faded brim, eyes peered defiantly at his audience. A straggly orange beard covered most of his thin face, his mouth a grim line. His tattered linen shirt sleeves were rolled up to expose wrists badly scarred, affirming the man had once been shackled.

"Cover your ears, Little One," Mary whispered as the constable seized the man's right hand, the hot iron just inches from the flesh. As Lizzie complied, Mary looked up at the man and her breath caught.

His eyes, as green as a meadow at dusk, were focused on her. She felt as though she was the only person in his line of vision, and his steady gaze unnerved her. Spellbound, she returned his gaze as the branding iron seared his right hand. Mary winced at the snakelike hiss of seared flesh, and she heard others around her moan in empathy. But the victim did not cry out. Only for a moment, torment flickered in his eyes, his whiskered jaw tensing while his face paled. His gaze remained intense, eyes glinting in the sun with defiant indignation.

The iron was withdrawn and the dreadful T, permanently burned into the man's hand, emitted a cloud of smoke. The smell of burnt flesh sickened Mary and she fought the urge to retch. Most victims fainted after being branded, but this man seemed intent on not succumbing to the pain. Constable Hart placed the brand in a bucket of water. The hot iron hissed again, sending a plum of steam up into the air. *Doling out punishment is always so difficult for Absalom,* Mary thought as her sympathy splintered between the victim and the punisher. *He looks as though he regrets his actions already.* Then her gaze returned to the pilloried man. His eyes were still focused on her.

"You shall remain in the pillory for two hours," her father intoned, looking directly at the thief. "After which time you will be escorted to the jail and detained until the High Sheriff collects you."

At her father's words, Mary managed to break free from the victim's penetrating gaze. Richard Case gave his daughter a curt nod, and she gently peeled Lizzie away from her. It fell upon her to dress the wound, and she retrieved the basket. Swallowing audibly, she approached the pilloried man while the crowd dispersed, the vials tinkling softly from within the swinging pouch. Constable Hart stepped aside, acknowledging Mary with his customary cheerlessness. She met the constable's gaze for a moment. His hooded dark eyes always held a look of melancholy that harbored a lifetime of sorrows. Next to the constable, young James stood awkwardly. His face appeared green after witnessing the branding.

This had not been the first time she'd had to tend to branding wounds, but something about this man unsettled her. He reeked of unwashed maleness and his eyes followed her every move as she set the basket down and opened the earthen pot of salve. She scooped a generous amount onto her fingers, then rose and reached for the fingers of the wounded hand.

The moment she touched those long, cool fingers, she felt as though a small lightning bolt had flowed from them straight through her body. She flushed hotly as she uncapped the crock of ointment, slathering it generously on the cauterized mark. She worked hastily, wanting to be gone from this man's disturbing presence. Wiping the greasy ointment from her fingers, she took up the linen strips and bound his entire hand.

"Bless you for this act of mercy," the thief mumbled in a voice so low she could barely hear it.

She glanced up at the remaining audience. Most of the townspeople had dispersed, but her father, Noah Parker, three magistrates and the constable remained.

"You mustn't speak to me," she hissed back, wrapping the linen slowly around the hand. When the thief's wound was dressed, Mary bent to retrieve her basket from the ground but discovered Constable

Hart had already done so. He held it out to her, touching the rim of his hat with his free hand. Mary accepted the basket with a quick nod. She was going to thank the constable when Noah Parker stepped up.

"Keep an eye out for his dog," Noah Parker said to Hart and his deputy, disregarding the pilloried man and taking Mary's arm possessively. "Tom Ellis said there was large black dog on his property when he apprehended this thief. Dog ran off afore he could fire a shot."

Mary glanced at Constable Hart, whose brooding dark eyes regarded the scene somberly. He was the captain of Hereford's local militia, and well-respected in the community. She knew little about Hart's personal life, but had heard rumors he'd witnessed the horrors of the Cocheco massacre in New Hampshire four years before. He was taller than both Richard and Noah, with a quiet, steadying air about him. Then Mary regarded Noah, once again noticing how small and beady his eyes were. Despite his being a minister, there was something untrustworthy about him. Looking into his bland face, she wondered again why Noah was so intent on marrying her. *Truly, there's no love between us,* she thought as she felt herself recoil at his touch. In truth, the only emotions Noah Parker evoked in Mary were irritation and a sense of distrust.

Richard Case seemed to dismiss the horrid branding spectacle, gesturing to draw both Noah and his daughters to him.

"Will you sup with us this evening, Noah?" He was saying, laying an arm on both Mary's and Noah's shoulders as if they were already united somehow.

"Why thank you, Reverend," the younger man said, smiling broadly. Mary took Lizzie's hand in hers, feeling her face grow hot again, but this time it was due to annoyance. "Until then, I'll retire to my room and prepare for the Sabbath's sermon."

The two ministers shook hands and Noah bowed courteously at Mary before striding across the courtyard to his own small dwelling. Adjacent to the rectory was a smaller clapboard house, the modest home of the assistant minister. It was a narrow, two-story structure with a sleeping loft in the garret. A casement window peered out across the courtyard like a Cyclops' eye, and sometimes Mary felt she was being watched, only to look up and see Noah in the window. The thought made her clench her teeth.

"Sister! You're hurting my hand!"

Mary released Lizzie's hand, suddenly aware of how tightly she was squeezing it. "I'm sorry, Lizzie. Go along now and tend to the hearth. I'll be right along."

As Richard and Lizzie headed towards the rectory, Mary shot a quick glance back at the pilloried man. He returned her gaze steadily until she looked away and followed her father and sister, walking past the few remaining stragglers of the audience.

"I heard he was in Salem's dungeon," Mary heard young James say as he passed her with the extinguished iron and water bucket. "His ma was one of them witches that nearly hanged."

This enticing bit of gossip stopped Mary, and she put a hand on James' arm. "Have you heard his name mentioned?" Mary pressed, wondering why that mattered to her.

The young man looked thoughtful as the green seemed to leave his freckled face. "David?" he spoke the name questioningly. "Nay, Daniel. I believe 'tis Daniel. Daniel Eames."

Mary released James' arm and glanced again at the thief, his name resonating in her head like an echo.

Daniel Eames.

Chapter Two

I knew not why that name should resonate with my soul so intensely, but upon hearing it I couldn't cease its refrain in my head. Dear Daughter, I believe it's because Providence meant for us to meet and produce you, our lovely Kezia. And for that, I have no regrets.

Noah Parker arrived an hour before supper. Lizzie and I tended to the stew pot while Father and Noah smoked their pipes on the front porch. I listened intently as their voices wafted in the warm evening air like pipe smoke.

"I hear this man Eames was imprisoned in Salem during that horrid business a year ago," Richard Case was saying.

"Aye," Noah confirmed. "As you know, I've an uncle in Salem. 'Twas from his very lips my father heard both he and his mother were tried for witchcraft but alas, were reprieved."

Intrigued, Mary leaned closer to the open window, stirring the stewpot silently. She met Lizzie's wide, anxious eyes and put a finger to her lips.

"Ah," Richard said. "How fares your uncle, now that he's no longer High Sheriff of that county?"

"He's partnered with his old chum, Will. They both left Salem after their involvements with the witch trials. When I heard the name of our resident thief, I penned a quick note to Uncle. They're both more than happy to bear witness against Eames. If the magistrates can arrange for a hearing within a week, the both of them should be able to attend and Will can put his talents to use after Eames is sentenced."

"But won't those duties fall to Hart?"

Mary heard Noah snort derisively. "Hart hasn't got the stomach to mete out righteous corporal punishment. Did you see how he hesitated at performing his duty this morn?"

Her father's low, rumbling chuckle chilled Mary, and she shivered despite the heat from the fire. *There's nothing wrong with a man having a sense of compassion*, she thought, and had a good mind to confront them. She gestured for Lizzie to fetch four gourd bowls, and she carefully ladled the thick stew into them. The men came inside, smelling of tobacco, and took their seats at the board. Richard took his place at the head of the board while Noah, being the guest of honor, sat at Richard's right. Mary and Lizzie sat below the salt, their heads bowed while they waited for their father to offer the blessing.

The meal was eaten quickly and silently, the stew and cornbread tasting as bland as sawdust in Mary's mouth. She dared not meet her father's nor Noah's eyes, and kept her head bent over her bowl. After the meal and evening prayers, she would carry the remains of the stew and bread to the jailhouse to share with Thomas Dirby, the aged jailer.

As the minister's daughter, the duty fell upon me to deliver victuals to the jailer and the incarcerated. With the jailhouse so near the meetinghouse and rectory, it was a short enough walk that the food was still warm. Lizzie and I walked across the courtyard, sharing the burden of the heavy kettle. To her credit, your Aunt Lizzie, dear child, exerted herself admirably, though the strain was evident on her small face. The basket of cornbread was tucked in the crook of her free arm, while in mine I carried an earthen jug of small beer. To this day, I shall always associate stew, cornbread, and small beer with the events of what happened next.

Mary rapped on the jailhouse door with the brass knocker. She heard Dirby's shuffling steps as he approached, and the heavy door opened, expressing an overpowering stench. Mary buried her nose into the crook of her arm and fought the urge to gag due to the stench of a wooden bucket nearly full of human waste placed near the door.

"Ain't had time to empty that slop bucket, my apologies," Dirby said, ambling back towards his desk. He was a thin and wiry old man with a club foot he dragged heavily across the pine wood floor.

Much of the time, the single cell in the small jailhouse was empty, and often Dirby was the only recipient of their leftovers. A dusty hearth made up one of the walls and appeared to have not been lit in some time. Dirby preferred to save his firewood for cooler weather. The jailer's narrow bed lay unkempt behind the desk. The cell was merely a fraction of the jailhouse, iron bars delineating it from the rest of the building. Mary's eyes refused to glance at the single inmate, but she knew he was sitting on the bare floor, his rope-bound wrists secured to a bolt in the wall.

"Empty that slop bucket, girlie," Dirby said to Lizzie, "Can't raise much of an appetite with such stink in the air."

Mary heard Lizzie sigh resignedly. This was often her job, if the bucket needed emptying. With disgust clear on her face, Lizzie released the stewpot's handle. Handing the basket to Dirby, she lifted the nasty slop bucket. Her eyes darted quickly to the prisoner, widening with fear before she averted her eyes and lugged the bucket out the door. Dirby left the door open behind her, to air out the small room before relieving her of the jug of beer and scurried to his desk. Unassisted, she dragged the stew pot across the floor with a noisy screech, leaving a distinct mark on the dusty floor. Her pouch swayed like a pendulum with each lumbering step.

"Smells good," Daniel Eames commented from the cell.

The sound of his voice raised gooseflesh on her arms, and she looked at Dirby, ravenously devouring his meal without offering a single prayer. He grunted his consent, and she broke off a piece of cornbread. She slipped it into the pouch that always dangled from her waist before she dragged the kettle to the cell.

A key ring with one large key hung on a nail near the cell door. Mary had only served inmates twice before, but this was the first time she felt so unsettled. Keeping her eyes lowered, she sprang the lock, returned the key to its nail and opened the creaking door. With difficulty, she dragged the stew pot closer to the prisoner. Kneeling beside him, she laid the cornbread in her lap and said, "Let us give thanks--"

Daniel Eames snorted so loudly she looked up, surprised by his disrespect. But the moment their eyes met, her breath caught in her throat. His eyes blazed with such hostility and derision she felt fearful, despite his being bound to the wall. His right hand was still covered in the bandage she'd wrapped, as starkly white as a deer's tail. His felt hat had tumbled to the dirt floor. It lay on its crown next to his long legs.

"A great lot I have to give thanks for," he scoffed.

She shot a quick glance at the jailer, still hunkered over his bowl of stew. Lizzie returned with the emptied bucket, and Mary called to her, "Fetch me the jug, Sister."

Lizzie obeyed, hoisting the jug from Dirby's desk. Her blue eyes again widened with trepidation as she regarded the prisoner. She set the jug down next to Mary and then retreated to the door. Mary knew her sister would wait outside until it was time to carry the kettle back to the rectory. Once Lizzie disappeared outside, Mary withdrew the ladle from the pot and lifted it to Daniel's mouth.

His eyes locked on hers, peering over the gourd ladle. She was mortified to see how much the ladle trembled in her hand, and stew trickled into the wiry orange whiskers on his chin. His prominent Adam's apple bobbed with each swallow, and at last he pulled his head away to chew on a piece of lamb. She withdrew the ladle and returned it to the pot.

"Wipe my chin," Daniel Eames instructed.

The intimacy of the requested act both shocked and thrilled her, and she felt compelled to comply. Lifting the corner of her apron, she dapped gently at his whiskers. He held her gaze steadily, and when she was finished, he said, "Tell me your name."

Despite the open door, the air seemed to be leaving the jailhouse and Mary found it hard to breathe. The sound of Daniel's low voice made her heart pound in her ears. He'd finished the stew and cornbread, and in her haste to leave him, she dropped the ladle into her lap. She felt herself blush hotly, feeling flustered and clumsy.

"I'm Mary, Reverend Case's daughter," she answered, watching him digest this information with the predatory thoughtfulness a snake gives a hapless rodent. "My sister and I will be bringing your meals once a day."

"Just you."

"Pardon?"

"Deliver my meals by yourself," he said. "That child's too fearful of me."

As am I! Mary wanted to say, but instead she brushed cornbread crumbs from her lap and stood. "Lizzie," she called in a quavering voice, "Take the jug and basket."

The little girl appeared in the doorway, approaching the cell like a skittish rabbit. Mary could see her sister's thin shoulders quaking and prayed she wouldn't have a seizure in the filthy cell. She handed the jug and basket to Lizzie and got to her feet. Daniel's concern for Lizzie's state of mind argued that Daniel had a sense of compassion, and Mary considered this quietly as she left the cell and locked the door behind her.

"Mary."

Startled to hear her name from his lips, she turned back to look at him, chained to the wall, but looking as cool as if he were lounging on a goose down mattress.

"See if tomorrow you can't scrounge me up some rum."

He grinned, flashed her haughty wink, and left her so flustered she forgot the stewpot.

Chapter Three

Father's words about him being imprisoned during those witch trials had me wondering if perhaps he was indeed a witch and had bespelled me, for after that first encounter, I could not shake the sensation of his lips on my fingers as I held out his bread. That night, I lay next to Lizzie, a tempest of thoughts in my head preventing sleep from overtaking me. Part of me dreaded our next encounter, while another part of me couldn't wait.

For the next two days, I brought the incarcerated man his daily sustenance. I became less fearful, and more intrigued whether I was in his presence or not. Sweet Lizzie was always my companion, for I trusted that with her there, nothing untoward would occur. Nonetheless, Daniel Eames made suggestive advances verbally, which appeared to go unnoticed by my innocent sister. Part of me, I confess, hoped she would leave us, if only for a moment. I'm quite positive it never occurred to her she was a sort of chaperone. And then came the evening of the Sabbath.

The next morning was Thursday and Mary went through her customary routine, her stomach queasy with anticipation. She stoked the hearth fire, and warmed a kettle of samp for the family's breakfast.

"What's wrong with your eyes, Sister?" Lizzie asked as she climbed the ladder from their loft. Lizzie always slept well, due to her morning and night doses of motherwort tincture.

"Sleep eluded me," she said simply, stirring the kettle. "Come, let's take your medicine."

Lizzie followed her obediently to the counter where the apothecary's flask sat next to the jugs of small beer, ale, cider and rum. The best the doctor could prescribe to combat Lizzie's fits was a foul-tasting motherwort tincture. Mary had become adept at measuring the correct dosage, and twice a day she and Lizzie went through this necessary ritual. She mixed the tincture with ale, since that was the combination Lizzie found most palatable. Once the little girl had downed her medicine, the rest of the morning routine would go on.

The day dragged on, anticipation and dread pecking at her heart like a persistent hen. Mary took her sewing basket outside and sat on the rectory's stoop. Her eyes often glanced up from her sewing, irresistibly drawn to the jailhouse. *There he sits,* she thought with a strange combination of anticipation and foreboding. *After the supper hour I'll see him yet again, and he'll send my heart racing with those green eyes of his.* She was twenty years old, and no man had ever conjured such excitement in her before. She wondered if he thought of her as often as she thought of him, and smiled at the concept.

A shadow fell across her lap, disturbing her musings. She glanced up to find Noah Parker standing next to her, holding a white linen shirt in his hand.

"Pray, mend this torn sleeve, would you?" he said, holding out the garment.

She exhaled, barely concealing her annoyance before she glanced up into his small, pasty face.

"Set it down and I'll have it finished before supper," she replied. *No doubt he'll sup with us this night, as always,* she thought glumly.

He tossed the shirt onto the stoop next to her and regarded the jailhouse thoughtfully before returning his beady eyes to her.

"It's unseemly, you taking that footpad his meals alone."

"I'm not alone, Noah." she defended. "The jailer's there."

He snorted derisively. "Why has Lizzie stopped accompanying you?"

"She's too affrighted."

He continued to peer at her beneath the brim of his hat with a keen sense of suspicion. "I've a mind to assign someone else to the task. Perhaps Goody Ellis or Goody Hawkins."

Mary sighed inwardly at the mention of the two matrons. "I've always brought Jailer Dirby his meals before, whether he had a prisoner in the cell or not."

Noah Parker shook his head. "Something about this miscreant unsettles me. I'll speak to the magistrates about it."

Mary knew better than to protest too much, so she fixed her eyes on her mending, jabbing the needle into the fabric. "Well, you can't speak to them 'til the morrow, so I daresay I can bring the fellow his sup tonight."

Noah's eyes narrowed. "Don't be insolent, Mary. I have a sermon to finish writing. After that, I'll escort you from the jailhouse."

Mary sighed in resignation. Squinting against the sun, she replied coldly, "It matters not to me what you do."

His mouth drew into an indignant line. "Have the shirt ready before the Sabbath," he ordered, then stomped back to his dwelling.

As soon as he walked away, Mary wanted to stick her tongue out at him, but instead dismissed him with a shake of her head. Her eyes strayed back to the jailhouse and her heart fluttered excitedly. All she could think of was seeing Daniel Eames again.

Sitting there with the jailhouse in view, I could only imagine what Daniel Eames was thinking, and wondered if he entertained any thoughts of me….

That evening, she and Lizzie brought baked beans with biscuits and creamed carrots. Lizzie carried the basket containing biscuits and a small crock of butter along with the rum jug. Mary carried the baked beans and carrots in their separate kettles. In her apron was tucked a ladle for serving, and a spoon with which to feed Daniel. Crossing the courtyard, they had to pass the stocks, whipping post and pillory, which always made Mary's stomach clench. She'd seen those implements used on several Hereford residents, and it seemed to her the cruel punishments did nothing to deter further sinful behavior.

She rapped on Dirby's door and listened for his shuffling footfalls. The little man opened the door with a perturbed expression until he recognized the rum jug. His old eyes brightened and he opened the door wider.

"Come in, come in!" he said, sidling up to his desk to await his meal. He rubbed his hairy hands in anticipation, his tankard and wooden trencher ready to receive her offerings.

Lizzie crept in beside her, already chewing on her coif strings. As soon as she deposited the basket and jug, Lizzie turned an anxious face to Mary.

"May I wait outside?" she asked in a small whisper.

"As soon as Jailer Dirby is served and you help me carry the food into the cell," Mary promised, then her eyes went to the prisoner in the cell.

"She brought rum, Eames!" Dirby exclaimed gleefully as he watched Lizzie pour the amber liquid into his tankard. The earthen jug was only half-full, and Dirby always favored the dregs. But Mary was careful to save some a few swallows for Daniel. Dirby's whiskered chin was wet with drool once the earthy aroma hit his nose. Lizzie handed him a biscuit and scooped a pat of butter from its crock. She flung the yellow glob onto his tankard while Mary served the beans and carrots.

"Huzzah!" Daniel exclaimed with mild enthusiasm. His eyes met Mary's with that cool glint that made her heart pound.

Once Dirby was happily devouring his meal, Mary took a deep breath and approached the cell. She felt Daniel watching her every movement as she reached for the key ring and unlocked the door.

"Good evening to you," she heard herself say, opening the door and carrying in the two kettles. She could sense Lizzie's fearful hesitation as the child followed behind with the basket and jug. She sat the kettles down next to the bound man and relieved Lizzie of her burden. "You may wait outside now, Sister," she said.

Lizzie's relief was so evident on her small face Mary had to smile. When the child departed, she knelt beside Daniel amidst the kettles, basket and jug. She saw that the ropes had begun to rub his scarred wrists raw and his hat still lay beside him on its crown.

"Let's give thanks--"

"Later," Daniel said gruffly. "Feed me now."

Mary flushed at the rude interruption and adjusted her position to more efficiently feed him. The vials in her pouch tinkled softly, and Daniel scowled with mild irritation.

"What's that in your purse?" he demanded.

Mary looked up, her mind not registering what he'd asked.

"In your pouch," he prompted. "It doesn't sound like coins."

Her right hand went protectively to the pouch before she explained quietly, "They're physicks for my sister. She has the falling sickness. One is to rouse her from her faints, the other is to quiet her mind and prevent the fits--"

She realized she was rambling, and a whole new wave of heat flushed her face. "May I offer you beans or carrots first?"

"First, a swig of that rum," he said.

Mary obliged, uncorking the rum jug and holding it to his mouth. He closed his eyes and swallowed loudly, looking as content as a nursing calf. When he was finished, she drew the jug away and he exhaled with a resounding belch. His eyes closed halfway and he seemed lost in a moment of bliss.

"Tell me about the physicks," he said as she lifted a spoonful of beans to his lips.

"The smaller one is hartshorn," she said, watching the spoon disappear past those lips. "The larger is motherwort tincture. She takes a morning and evening dose to help her sleep and ward off the fits."

His eyes settled thoughtfully on the pouch dangling at her waist. "Motherwort tincture," he repeated.

"Mary!"

She jumped at the sound of Noah Parker's voice, dropping a

spoonful of carrots into her lap. Annoyance darkened Daniel's face and she felt a degree of irritation too as she wiped at the spilled carrots before looking over her shoulder at Noah. He stood in the open doorway of the little jailhouse. She knew he never set foot in the small building because the pervasive stench was too offensive to his senses. He wore the same spotless white scarf and tall-crowned hat as he always did, his face stern with disapproval.

"Your father sent me to fetch you. You're taking too long."

"But he hasn't finished--"

"He's had enough," Noah interrupted her, drawing his scarf over his sensitive nose and gesturing impatiently with his free hand. "I sent Lizzie on home. I'll carry the kettles for you."

"Then come in and fetch them yourself, you dandy."

At Daniel's defiant challenge, Mary's jaw dropped, but she snapped it shut before an amused chuckle escaped her. She bit her lip as she got to her feet and watched an indignant Noah drop his scarf. He drew a deep breath from outside before entering the jailhouse as if he were charging into battle. He helped her stand and took up the two kettles, leaving the jug and basket for her to take. While Noah was just a foot away from the bound man, Daniel lunged forward as far as he could, causing Noah to flinch. Noah's doughy face reddened as he continued to hold his breath and he bolted out of the cell with Daniel's laughter in his wake. Mary heard Noah release his breath in one great gush once he was outside.

As Mary exited the cell, she lowered her head so that Dirby wouldn't see her face as locked the cell door behind her. She stood facing Daniel again. With Dirby's back to her, she succumbed and the corners of her mouth lifted. Daniel met her smile with a cool wink.

"Mary! Come along now!"

At Noah's impatient beckoning, she tore herself away and joined him in the courtyard. The summer evening air was alive with animal sounds in the nearby forest and heavily scented with the dense flora. The sun blazed orange through the trees and a thrill of exhilaration skittered up and down Mary's spine until Noah spoke.

"I'll be escorting you on your duties to the jailhouse until I can arrange for one of the matrons to take over."

"I received word Uncle George and his partner will attend Eames' hearing," Noah was saying casually. "They'll make solid witnesses for the prosecution."

Mary stopped sweeping abruptly, staring at her father and Noah as they hunkered over the large Bible on the board. It was Friday, and the two ministers were putting finishing touches on Sunday's sermon. Parchment was a precious commodity, and Reverend Case wrote his sermons in pencil. Each week, he would ball up a wad of soft bread and erase the old writing to make room for the next. For this reason, Mary's weekly bread baking occurred on Monday, unlike most households, who baked on Saturdays.

While Mary swept, Lizzie had left the house with the bucket of food scraps to toss into the trees.

"With the combined testimony of Hereford's own good citizens, I'm certain that scoundrel will hang for his crimes," Noah added.

Mary felt as though her blood had frozen in her veins. She knew any commentary from her was unwanted, and she gripped the broom handle so tightly her knuckles blanched against her skin. Both men looked at her with mild irritation.

"Make haste and finish your chores, Daughter!" Richard ordered. "You have little time before prayers to take Dirby his sup."

Mary was about to speak when the quiet afternoon was shattered by a terrified scream.

"That's Lizzie!" Mary cried, dropping the broom. It clattered to the floor as both men rose from the board and hurried outside. Mary followed, the pouch pouncing against her hip.

To the west of the rectory a dense copse of trees grew, obscuring the view of the Great River beyond. Lizzie stood trembling on the fringe of the tree line, the scrap bucket lying at her feet with vegetable parings spilling from it. Mary ran to her sister. Kneeling in front of the girl, she put her hands on Lizzie's quaking shoulders. The men joined them, standing by helplessly as Mary looked intently into the child's eyes.

"Lizzie, Lizzie, look at me," she demanded in a firm voice.

But it was too late. Lizzie's eyes rolled into her head, and she began to convulse. Noah caught her before her legs buckled, and he carried the seizing child into the house.

Noah deposited Lizzie gingerly on her trundle bed. Mary's vision blurred with tears as they always did when her sister was in the throes of a fit. She removed the little girl's coif and stroked the damp hair, cooing soothingly. Richard and Noah stood off to the side, as useless as damp kindling. Familiar with the routine, they waited until the seizure passed, and Lizzie lay still, pale and sobbing.

"What frightened you, Sister?" Mary asked softly, still stroking the girl's hair.

Fat tears rolled down Lizzie's little face and her mouth contorted into a lopsided pout. "A dog," she said finally. "A great big one. It just sat there, watching me from the tree line. At first I thought it was a bear, and then I felt the fit come upon me and I couldn't move."

"Can you describe the dog?" Noah Parker asked from the foot of the bed.

"Black and shaggy," Lizzie replied, sniffling.

"Could be the very beast seen accompanying Eames," Noah speculated.

Mary swallowed, fighting a surge of panic. "Lizzie needs to rest and I've yet to take Dirby his victuals," she said. "May I go do that now, Father?"

"Aye, Daughter," Richard replied, "but as I said before, make haste. Attend to her, Noah."

Mary hastily packed her basket with bread and a small crock of apple butter. Noah carried the ale jug and kettle of samp across the courtyard for her. With every step as they neared the jailhouse, Mary resented his presence more and more.

"You're late," Dirby grumbled, opening the door for her and relieving her of the basket and jug.

"Lizzie's unwell," Mary explained shortly, her eyes already on Daniel as the wizened jailer attacked his meal. She went to unlock the cell door while Noah hung back just outside the door.

"I see you found another girl to assist you," Daniel smirked, glancing at Noah.

"Be civil, Eames," Noah shot back, his scowl looking more like an indignant child's pout.

Daniel gestured obscenely with his good hand, and Mary lowered her head as she turned to face Noah. He looked righteously offended and his face flushed red. The corners of her mouth twitched at Daniel's boldness and she bit her lips to suppress a laugh.

With her back to Noah and Dirby, Mary released her smile to Daniel. As she entered the cell, Daniel grew serious and asked, "What ails your sister?"

"She mistook a large dog for a bear and the fear drew forth one of her fits," Mary explained in a whisper as she arranged herself next to him.

Daniel asked sharply, "A black dog?"

She nodded, opening the crock of apple butter. "Aye. They suspect it belongs to you, and are on the lookout for it."

They both glanced quickly at Noah, who watched them from the doorway. Mary took a deep breath and whispered, "Father said your trial begins the day after Sabbath. Some men from Salem are coming to testify against your character."

Confusion furrowed Daniel's brow and his Adam's apple bobbed in his throat. "What men?"

"Noah Parker's uncle," she said, picking up on a vague sense of panic. "I heard Noah say he was once High Sheriff of--"

"Essex County?"

"I know not," she stammered.

"Who travels with him?" Daniel demanded, straining against the iron tether.

The fierce look in his eye frightened her, and she almost considered calling out to Dirby.

"I believe his first name is Will...."

Confirmation was replaced by sheer rage as he struggled against his constraints. Dread chilled Mary as she realized these men truly presented a threat to Daniel.

"Mary, let's be off," Noah commanded from the open doorway.

"I know who they are," Daniel said in a low voice. "And they will see me hang."

She felt like she was inside a giant bell and the clapper had just struck. His words reverberated in her head so loudly she couldn't think straight. She shook her head to clear it and heard her own voice say, "I want to help."

She wasn't sure she'd spoken the thought aloud until she saw hope flicker in his eyes before they were once again eclipsed by desperation. She was certain Noah couldn't have heard her words as he glared at them from the doorway. And Dirby was too obtuse to have ever noticed.

"Mary!" Noah called again impatiently.

"Then help me escape," Daniel said to her, his feral green eyes boring into her. "Soon."

She heard Noah's boots on the floorboards, coming towards them. She suddenly felt dizzy and her head began to pound.

Scrambling to her feet, she whispered breathlessly, "I will."

Chapter Four

Moonlight was beginning to replace the waning sun, and Mary was so lost in her own thoughts she was barely aware of Noah's presence. He carried the samp kettle in his left hand while grasping her elbow with his right, guiding her forcefully as they strode across the courtyard. She resented his touch and resisted the urge to pull her arm free, but instead she ignored his ramblings. Her head was still throbbing as thoughts swirled within it. *Why did I say I would help him?* Her mind demanded. *Now the poor man is counting on me!* Meanwhile, her heart screamed, *and what can I do? How can I possibly help him escape? I can't have someone else deliver the victuals to him! If only I could help him escape this very night--*

She was jolted from her reverie when Noah stopped short just as they passed the pillory, stocks and whipping post. He pointed at the tree line. "Look there! Do you see it?"

She scowled. It was sunset and there were too many shadows to make out anything clearly. She was suddenly fearful of attack and whispered back, "What is it, a wolf?"

"Nay," Noah replied, grinning sardonically. "'Tis Eames' beast. It's been seen skulking about. It must know its vile master lies in the jailhouse. We've set snares for it, but alas, no luck as yet."

The quick flare of rage Mary felt surprised her. She took great offense at how he insulted Daniel. For a moment she felt like hurtling the ale jug at his head, but instead she clenched the handle until her knuckles were as pale as the earthen vessel itself.

Noah resumed their walk across the courtyard, escorting her to the rectory door. Finally releasing her elbow, he said, "I bid you good night, and I trust you will sleep well knowing you no longer carry that loathsome burden any longer."

She looked up into his square, pasty face, looking even paler in the dimming light. *It was neither loathsome nor a burden!* She wanted to argue. Instead, she smiled demurely and croaked out a wooden, "Thank you. Good night, Noah."

He set the kettle down while she opened the rectory door. Once the door was opened, she took the kettle and disappeared inside, glad to be rid of his company.

Her father sat at the hearth reading aloud while Lizzie sat like an attentive but tired cherub. She quietly excused herself before relieving Mary of the basket and jug.

"You took far too long," accused Richard, blowing a puff of smoke into the room. "'Tis past time for Elizabeth's medicine. Then it's prayers before bed."

"Aye, Father," Mary replied automatically, her mind still a flurry of confusion, fear and excitement. She hung the samp kettle on a pot hook in the hearth. "Come, Lizzie."

Under the warm glow of candlelight, Mary performed the nightly ritual of preparing Lizzie's tincture. The apothecary's bottle was kept next to the jugs of ale, rum, cider and small beer. Mary mixed it with ale while Lizzie stood next to her. The child's doleful little face peered up at her beneath her coif, already grimacing at the prospect of downing the awful medicine.

Poor Lizzie, Mary thought again, watching her sister guzzle the foul drink as quickly as she could. *But at least the physick brings about sound sleep.*

Many nights, when she couldn't sleep, Mary would work on her sewing until her eyes grew weary. She had intended to make use of the bright moonlight and sit by the opened window. Her eye fell on her sewing basket. Her small knife, used mainly for cutting herbs from the garden, nestled atop a pile of folded linen.

Lizzie handed her the emptied cup, shaking her head violently and sticking her tongue out. Mary set the cup next to the trio of earthenware jugs, her eyes lingering on the one containing the dregs of rum. Slowly an idea began to form.

"Prayers now, Daughters." Richard said, tapping the pipe bowl against the hearth before he placed it in its box.

She walked as if in a dream to the hearth as she and Lizzie positioned themselves for prayers. It was difficult to conceal the excitement rising within her, and she could barely contain the urge to fidget as Richard intoned the nightly prayers. Richard's pipe smoke lingered, sweetening the stagnant air.

"Father," she said after prayers were finished, "I'm not yet sleepy and I've some sewing to finish. I'll be to bed as soon as I can."

Richard seemed pleased that his daughter was so industrious, and rose from his seat. "Then good night to you, Daughter." He said.

Lizzie's eyelids were already drooping, and she kissed both Richard and Mary on the cheek before climbing the staircase to the loft she and Mary shared. Richard retired to his own room, and she sat quietly, gazing into the glowing embers in the hearth. She listened for her father's snoring before she tucked her little knife into her stays. Then she crept silently across the room to the rum jug. Only the last dregs remained, and she was careful not to slosh the contents. She uncorked the jug as silently as she could and uncapped the tincture bottle. She wished she could muffle the sounds of liquid echoing into the jug as she added a healthy measure of tincture. Recapping both vessels, she tucked the jug under her arm. Clutching the velvet pouch to her to prevent the vials from tinkling she plucked her linen cloak from its hook. She threw it over her shoulders and pulled the hood over her head, trembling with fear and excitement. Then as stealthily as she could, she opened the rectory door and stepped into the pale moonlight.

This is madness! Her mind screamed, and she felt weirdly detached, as if she were a passive observer to her own actions.

Crickets sang loudly and she heard a wolf howl somewhere in the trees. Closing the door softly behind her, Mary took a deep breath. The pillory, stocks and whipping post mocked her ghoulishly, challenging her to cross the courtyard alone. Her heart beat wildly and she felt as if she were standing on the edge of a cliff. She shivered in the night air and drew her cloak tightly around her before she sprinted towards the jailhouse.

"Jailer, open up!" She whispered hoarsely, afraid to use the knocker. "I've brought you some rum!"

After a moment she heard the old man stir, dragging his club foot as he crossed the room. He unlocked the door and peered at her in confusion. Before he could question her, Mary held up the rum jug.

"Father said to give you the dregs before I refill this with new rum," she whispered, smiling brightly.

Dirby scratched his chin. His night cap was askew, and he squinted past her. "You brought it alone, in the dark?"

Mary nodded vigorously, almost shaking off her hood. "Never fear! With this moon, it's like daylight."

The old man looked at the rum jug, his interest clearly piqued. Never one to question free rum when it was offered, he threw back the door and ushered her in. "Well then, come in!"

The moonlight penetrated the darkness from the open doorway, and Dirby left it open so she could see to pour the rum. Her eyes darted quickly to Daniel's cell. He was watching her intently, his eyes glinting in the moonlight. The white bandage on his injured hand seemed to flicker like a candle flame.

"None for you, Eames!" Dirby bellowed as he wrung his hands in obvious anticipation. Mary smiled graciously and emptied the jug into his waiting tankard. The old jailer downed the treat in a series of noisy gulps, then returned the emptied tankard to his desk and belched loudly. He swayed slightly and grabbed the edge of his desk for support. "Drank it too fast, methinks," he slurred woozily.

"Then lie down," Mary suggested, taking Dirby's arm and leading him gently to his cot. "I'll show myself out."

"You're a kind lass," Dirby mumbled, leaning against her and blowing his foul breath into her face. He allowed himself to be deposited on his thin cot, and collapsed into an unconscious heap.

"Jailer?" Mary called softly, and tried rousing him by shaking his shoulder. When Dirby didn't respond, she took a deep breath, strode purposefully across the room and retrieved the key ring from its hook.

"Sly wench!" Daniel smiled approvingly as she opened the cell door and tossed the keys carelessly on the floor. "I wasn't sure I could trust you."

"You can trust me," she replied, unsheathing her little knife and plying it to the ropes, careful to aim the blade skyward. "I'm a minister's daughter."

He released an amused snort at this, and the moment the ropes were severed, he flexed his arms and rolled his shoulders. In a single swift move, he snatched his hat from the floor and was on his feet, towering above her still-kneeling form. He offered her his left hand, which she accepted. He helped her stand, and she stammered for something to say. Returning her little knife to its sheath she held it out to him. Her hand was trembling so much she almost dropped it. "Take this. It's small but sharp."

He released her hand, accepted the knife and tucked it into his boot. Then he hooked his arm around her waist and drew her closer. Before she could think, his mouth was on hers, and she felt like she'd fall into an abyss if he let her go. The kiss was her first, and though she had nothing to compare it to, she couldn't imagine a more intoxicating experience. Just as quickly, he released her, leaving her dazed and breathless.

"Go now afore you are missed," he told her gruffly, his words barely penetrating the roaring in her ears. "I'll watch that you make it back to the rectory."

She nodded stupidly, her face flushing hotly. Her hood had fallen off, and she pulled it back over her head before they both exited the cell. Dirby still lay motionless on his cot, and they both paused in the open doorway. He gave her a slight nudge and she darted blindly across the courtyard, dodging the implements of punishment.

I've done it! Her heart cried gleefully. *But what have I done?* Her mind argued. *Surely his escape will rouse suspicion upon me….*

She reached the rectory door, her heart pounding like hoof beats. She took a moment to collect herself, and took a deep breath. *Compose yourself,* she scolded, reaching for the doorknob. *What's done can't be undone.*

"Mary."

Her racing heart froze as large hands seized her shoulders and spun her around. Before she could cry out, a hand clamped firmly over her mouth and she found herself eye to eye with Noah Parker, his face a mask of disbelief and outrage.

Chapter Five

"Mary!" Noah hissed, his hand still clamped over her mouth. "Hush or you'll wake your father. What are you doing out here alone?"

How much had he seen? What does he know? Mary's mind questioned, fear and confusion muddling her thoughts. Although her heart still beat wildly, Mary scowled and with her free hand pulled his away from her mouth. Remembering the rum jug, she said pointedly, "I was delivering dregs of rum to Dirby. It's nearly daylight, as bright as the moon is--"

"You're not to deliver anything alone to the jailhouse while that thief Eames is there," Noah said as if he were scolding a naughty child. Then realization illuminated his large face. "You went to visit Eames, didn't you?"

Mary opened her mouth to speak, only to hear a voice from behind Noah say, "That she did."

Noah's face blanched before a hand clamped on his shoulder and spun him around. Before Noah could react, a fist bore into his square, pasty face, and he collapsed at Mary's feet. The rum jug fell from Mary's hand, hitting the ground with a hollow *thud*. Daniel Eames' tall, lanky form stood before her, bathed in the pale moonlight.

"What did you do?" Mary asked in an anxious whisper.

He held out a hand to her. "You need to come with me," he said.

He wants me to leave with him! Her heart sang at the romance of it. But her dutiful mind made her say, "I can't leave Lizzie."

"You have no choice," Daniel argued, his hand still stretched out to her. "They'll know 'twas you that helped me escape."

"Mayhap Dirby won't remember--"

"Dirby's why you need to come with me," Daniel insisted, the desperation in his eyes chilling her. "I checked on him after you left. He's dead."

I had committed the grievous sin of murder! However unintentional, the old jailer was dead due to my actions. Before I could register this information properly, Daniel grabbed my hand and we fled across the courtyard and into the dense woods. I felt as though I were running in a dream, low tree limbs reaching out like skeletal hands to catch me. To say there wasn't an exhilarating thrill to this would be a lie, but my rational mind screamed, what have I done?

He dragged her through the forest, low tree branches and brambles scratching her face and catching her skirts. She tripped on tree roots and stumbled over rocks, with only an impatient yank on her arm to keep from falling. When they came to the river bank, Daniel paused, still clutching Mary's hand.

"Riff!" he called, letting out a shrill whistle.

From the shadows, a large black dog bounded towards them. Obviously overjoyed to be reunited with his master, the dog placed his forepaws on Daniel's shoulders and began smothering him in slobbery dog kisses, whining softly. Daniel pushed the dog down, and the happy creature acknowledged Mary with a friendly sniff.

"What about my sister? She needs me--"

Daniel hastily removed the bandage from his seared hand, the T glaring red and angry against his skin. Flinging the white cloth on the ground, he began frantically pushing aside broken tree limbs and brambles, exposing a small canoe lying belly-up. "I used this canoe to get to Hereford in the first place," he explained. "Got it off an Indian. Now help me carry this to the river."

"But my sister--"

Only then did he turn his cold, desperate face to hers. "Mary," he said, holding up his branded hand, "I am an escaped fugitive. You are my accomplice and a murderess. You can never come back to Hereford."

At last the shock began to wear off, and her eyes flooded with tears. She repeated the word "*murderess*" to herself, and suddenly felt ill. She buried her face in her hands and wept. *What have I done? Dear Lizzie will be lost without me! And poor Dirby!*

"Help me!"

At Daniel's insistent whisper, Mary obeyed, sniffling and wiping her eyes as they hoisted the canoe onto their shoulders. Daniel retrieved a single paddle from beneath the little craft and they headed toward the river. Moonlight shimmered on the wide stretch of water like a magical path, and together they glided the canoe into the water. Apparently unaware of the seriousness of their situation, Riff bounded gleefully into the boat, wagging his massive tail. She stood at the water's edge, uncertain what to do. The peal of the church bell from the center of town caused her to jump.

"We're discovered," Daniel said. "Get in this canoe or, by God, I'll throw you in it myself."

Still sobbing, Mary waded into the mucky river. Water seeped into her shoes, chilling her feet and wetting the hems of her skirts. She climbed clumsily into the boat next to Riff, who gave her a welcoming sniff before Daniel pushed the wooden craft into the water. The canoe bobbed and wobbled, and Mary clutched the sides as Daniel jumped in. She'd heard many stories of white settlers being abducted by Indians, sailing away in canoes such as this, but she hadn't resisted, and Daniel's argument made sense; she could not return to Hereford.

Something in the water splashed near the side of the boat, and she jumped. She wanted to ask if he had some sort of plan, but instead she withdrew into her cloak, shivering and wiping away tears. She looked up at him as he expertly paddled the canoe, gliding silently across the band of water. *I don't know him,* she realized. *He could murder me this minute, and throw me overboard.*

"Don't be afraid of me," Daniel said as if reading her thoughts. "I won't hurt you."

As if to express his master's sentiment, Riff rested his massive head on Mary's lap and looked up at her with the unfailing trust only a dog could give. The shadowy figure of a wolf emerged briefly from the trees, then disappeared again. Mary shivered. Finally she managed to ask, "Where are we going?"

"South."

It seemed unlikely Daniel was going to elaborate, so Mary sat rigidly in the canoe, absently stroking Riff's head. She gazed at the full beauty of the pale moon until it transformed into Lizzie's sweet, trusting face.

Forgive me, Little One! Mary pleaded silently. *I never meant to abandon you.* Her hand fell on the velvet pouch dangling at her waist. She turned fretfully to Daniel.

"I'm the only one who knows how to administer Lizzie's medicine!" she gasped. "Father doesn't know--"

"He can ask the apothecary," Daniel replied smoothly.

"She needs an exact dose, morning and night!" Her panicked voice caused Riff to raise his head from her lap, and she clutched the edges of the boat. "Oh, take me back! Poor Lizzie!"

Without stopping his rhythmic paddling, Daniel said, "There is no going back. I told you before."

O how I wept for my little sister! She would awake to find me gone, and that shock alone could send her into a fit! Suddenly I hated this man for bespelling me in such a way that I would abandon sweet Lizzie! It was because of him Lizzie's heart would break as it did when Mother died. It was because of him the old jailer was dead. But no, I realized it was due to my own actions, and I sobbed with bitter regret until I slumped exhausted in the canoe, floating helplessly down the Great River to a fate I couldn't imagine.

Chapter Six

While we drifted steadily downriver, our absence was quickly discovered. My thoughts remained only on Lizzie. O Daughter, if I could only have realized the full extent of my actions, I would hopefully have acted more wisely. I was told later what happened in my absence....

"Reverend Case! Let me in!"

Richard Case awoke groggily to heavy pounding on the rectory door. He wondered vaguely why Mary hadn't answered, and grumbled to himself as he pulled on his breeches and unlatched the door. He opened it to find Noah Parker standing on his stoop, his nose bloodied and lying off-center in his doughy face. "Noah! What--?"

"Eames has escaped somehow, and I think he took Mary," Noah explained, his voice sounding nasal and whiny. "I saw her coming from the jailhouse with a jug of rum. I chastised her for going out without an escort, and last thing I knew, I was out. I think Eames struck me--"

Richard stared at Noah in disbelief. "Don't be ridiculous. Surely she's asleep. *Mary!*" Richard bellowed, the single word echoing through the small rectory. "Mary, come down here at once."

Both men heard stirring up in the loft, and soon Lizzie appeared on the stair, her eyes bleary from sleep. "Mary's not up here, Papa."

Richard ran a hand over his face. "Go wake Constable Hart," he ordered Noah. "The magistrates will need to be informed immediately.

Then send Goody Ellis to tend to Lizzie." To Lizzie, he said, "Be a brave girl and latch the door behind me. Open it only when Goody Ellis arrives. I will be back as soon as I can."

"Where's Mary, Papa?" Lizzie asked, already trembling.

"I don't have time for one of your fits," Richard barked. "Do as I say and latch the door behind me."

He rarely spoke harshly to Lizzie, and her little face crumbled at his words, but Reverend Case had no patience for childish tears, and he closed the door behind him, prodding Noah with an elbow. They both scurried in different directions, Noah to fetch the constable and Richard to the jailhouse.

"Open up, Dirby!" he demanded, pounding on the door. When Dirby didn't answer, he tried the latch. The door opened effortlessly, and he gasped at what he saw. Dirby lay pale and motionless on his cot, and beyond him, the empty cell door gaped open. All that remained in the cell were the remnants of severed rope that had once bound Eames' wrists. The key ring lay forgotten on the floor, yet there seemed to be no signs of struggle.

He has taken my daughter! Richard realized. Anger and disbelief wrestled for dominance in his head as he fled across the courtyard to the meetinghouse. Once inside, he seized the bell ropes and pulled furiously, summoning all who could hear to gather immediately.

By the time the townsmen and magistrates assembled, the sun was just beginning to rise. Richard paced the aisle, fighting off disturbing mental images of his daughter being carried off to an unknown fate. Finally, he sat at the pulpit with his head in his hands while Constable Hart and magistrates discussed what to do.

"We've examined the jailhouse," Constable Hart was saying, holding his hat in his massive hands. "Eames could not have cut his own ropes nor unlocked the cell without an accomplice." Looking almost apologetically at Richard, he said, "It appears your daughter opened the door and freed him herself."

At this, Richard's head shot up angrily. "Don't be absurd! He had an accomplice, surely, but if it were Mary, she wouldn't have aided him willingly--"

"When she brought him his meals, I often heard the two of them whispering," Noah supplied. "Mayhap they contrived this act together--"

Richard glared at his assistant minister. "How dare you make such accusations? Clearly Mary is some kind of hostage--"

"If she is a hostage," a new voice said from the back of the room, "we'll find her."

Noah turned towards the voice and smiled, traces of blood still on his face. "Uncle George!" Everyone turned to see two strangers make their way towards the pulpit. Noah rose and embraced his uncle, then shook the hand of the dark, stocky man beside him. "Everyone, may I present my Uncle George Corwin, formerly High Sheriff of Essex County, and his partner, William Dounton."

Quick introductions were made, and Corwin seated himself among the magistrates, clearly taking charge of the room. Dounton remained standing, observing the room with cold, beady eyes that made Richard shiver. Corwin removed his hat and held it in his lap. "I trust your county sheriff has been informed."

"We sent a courier soon as we heard," replied Constable Hart, his voice icy with indignation.

"I'll have Eames here and on the gallows before sundown," Corwin blustered. "We brought dogs in the event of this very situation."

"How could you have known Eames would escape before his trial?" Constable Hart asked.

Corwin smiled wryly. "Because," he said, "I know Eames."

At one point, Mary had either fainted or succumbed to sleep. She found herself curled in the bottom of the canoe, Riff licking her tear-streaked face. Disoriented, she blinked, pushing the dog's snout away. The sun was just rising above the treetops and the air had the freshness of morning. The craft lurched beneath her, and she looked up to find Daniel pulling the little vessel up onto the river bank. She felt stiff and sore, and sat for a moment to collect her bearings.

"We're here," Daniel said. "Help me secure this canoe."

Riff jumped out of the vessel, darting away from his master, and then returning with such unabashed glee Mary almost smiled. Then she remembered Lizzie, waking up to find herself abandoned. Propping herself up, she said, "I must get back to my sister." Her throat was dry and her voice was hoarse and cracked.

Daniel's only reply was to extend his left hand. Instinctively, she took it and crawled awkwardly out of the canoe. He remained silent until the boat was again belly-up on the river bank. "Please!" she persisted, hating the whine in her voice, "Lizzie needs me--"

He turned to face her with such a hard look she recoiled. "I won't repeat this again. There is no going back."

"But Lizzie--"

"I'm tired, and I'm hungry," Daniel snarled back. "If you want to return so badly, go ahead."

Mary stomped her foot in frustration, ashamed of the hot tears that threatened to leak from her eyes. "We don't even know where we are!"

"I do."

This didn't surprise her that much. Daniel seemed to be following some sort of plan. Tears and snot trickled down her face and she swiped at them with her apron. He watched her for a moment before his face softened and he touched her arm. "Sometimes the best thing you can do for family is leave them."

Mary felt like her rib cage was tightening, and she couldn't get a deep breath. She jerked her arm away and cocooned herself in her cloak. "Don't touch me," she muttered, her resentment towards him rising.

He dropped his hand, seemingly unconcerned about her distress, and began trudging up the steep embankment. Apparently oblivious to the tension between the man and woman, Riff trotted alongside his master, wide pink tongue lolling to one side. She had no choice but to follow them, so she picked up her sodden skirts and clambered up the river bank after them, grasping at rocks and low tree branches for support. Her anger at this man and at herself rose with every step, and when they got to the top of the bank, she refused his proffered hand. Struggling clumsily, she dusted off her skirts before rising to her full height. He gave her an unapologetic look, and she was about to tell him to go to the Devil when she looked past his shoulder and screamed.

Behind him stood a bare-chested Algonquin warrior.

Chapter Seven

"*Miskwandibe.*"

As the warrior addressed him, Daniel turned around casually. Riff looked questioningly from Mary to the Indian, and then at Daniel, who said, "Ho, Charles."

The warrior wore only a breechclout, his arms and chest adorned with tattoos. He held a musket in his lean arms. A roach headdress protruded stiffly from his shaved scalp and a powder horn and shot bag dangled from his beaded belt. He regarded Mary with eyes as dark as a starless night sky.

Mary watched dumbfounded as the Indian approached and the two men shook hands. Her empty stomach lurched and she felt sick. Defenseless, she drew her cloak tighter around herself, wishing she at least had her little knife, which poked out from Daniel's right boot. Riff sauntered up to the Indian, sniffing the tawny bare legs. Mary hadn't moved, and Daniel gestured for her to come closer.

"Mary, come meet Charles. He won't hurt you."

She felt as if she'd taken root. She was so terrified she couldn't move. Daniel scowled at her and said, "Come here!"

I've become a hostage! her mind screamed. *He is going to sell me to this Indian! I'll be made a slave, and I'll never see Lizzie again!*

Daniel strode towards her, grabbing her arm and dragging her closer to where the Indian stood watching them, as expressionless as a tree. She was too fearful to look into the warrior's broad face, and lowered her head, focusing on the tops of her ruined shoes.

"Don't be rude," Daniel said, releasing her arm. He said something to the Indian, who gave Mary a disdainful look before he turned away from them and trudged confidently into the woods.

"How do you know--" she whispered.

"His name is Chansomps," Daniel interrupted. "But I call him Charles. He calls me Miskwandibe. That means Red Hair." Daniel glanced at her. "I knew this is where his village would be. He probably saw us coming after that last bend in the river."

"But why--"

"We met two years ago. He thinks I saved his son's life."

Mary blinked, wondering if she'd misheard. "He *thinks?*"

Daniel lowered his voice and gave her an almost sheepish look. "In truth, 'twas Riff who saved the boy from a bear attack. I got there just in time to save Riff, but Charles here arrived just as I slew the bear." Daniel smiled wryly. "The child was too small to tell Charles what truly happened, and Riff…well, he keeps secrets good. That was the last time Providence smiled upon me, until last night when you helped me escape."

And why did I do that? Daughter, I asked myself that a million times, and a million times I cursed my own vulnerable heart for having led me astray. At that moment, whatever I felt for Daniel Eames had dissolved, and I felt as trapped as an unfortunate fly in a spider's web. Somehow I would find a means of escape, I vowed. And then I remembered, my past life no longer existed. I couldn't continue on my happy path as though nothing had happened. I could dismiss that life easier were it not for Lizzie. I prayed for her fragile body and her unhealthy mind. Moreover, I prayed that she wouldn't grow to hate me.

They entered a wide clearing dotted by a cluster of bark-covered wigwams. The domed structures were arranged like a colony of ant-hills, and Charles led them through a maze of cooking fires and racks where fish and venison were being smoked. Delicious smells from steaming kettles made Mary's stomach rumble. Two women looked up from the bear hide they were scraping and looked at Mary's cloaked form with disapproval. One of them made a rude sound and the other laughed before they both resumed their scraping.

Children darted out to greet them, chattering happily. They patted Riff, whose tail wagged continuously. Then they peered at Mary, whispering and giggling to each other until Charles ordered them away with gentle words. From the crowd an old man appeared, his face as brown and wrinkled as a walnut. His head was shaved like Charles', but his body was old and shriveled. He greeted Daniel with a toothless smile and Daniel said to Mary, "This is Eluwilussit, the sachem. I call him Eli."

Mary cocooned herself in her cloak. Charles seemed to comment on Daniel's branded hand, and he explained his mistreatment to them in their own tongue. Eli led them into a small, insignificant wigwam that smelled like smoke and old deer hides. They ducked their heads to enter the low doorway, and Mary covered her nose with her cloak, fighting the urge to gag as she seated herself on a folded blanket next to Daniel. Riff sauntered into the wigwam carrying a raw deer leg. He curled up behind Daniel and began devouring the treat with happy growls. She thought absently that some child probably offered it to the hungry dog as she ran her hand nervously across the rough woolen blanket. She felt like she'd stepped into a dream and that her real life, her old life, had fallen away.

Daniel, Charles and Eli seemed to forget about her and began talking. Suddenly someone nudged her shoulder, and she looked up, startled to see a young Indian woman offering her a slice of cornbread and a bowl of beans. Mary nodded her thanks and poked at the food delicately, although she was famished. She ate quietly while the men talked and ate; glad to be forgotten for a moment. The men's mirthful laughter frightened her even more. *Mayhap I can escape at night while the others are asleep,* she considered briefly. But even if she managed to set the canoe into the river, she knew nothing about how to maneuver it, and where would she go? Even if she fought the current and managed to return to Hereford, she would be hanged for Dirby's murder and her part in Daniel's escape. She contemplated going further downriver, to the nearest settlement she came across, and beg to be taken in.

"Mary," Daniel said, disturbing her reverie with a slight elbow nudge. "They want to know who you are."

They were all eating and drinking, and seemed quite relaxed. Charles and Eli looked at her expectantly, as if they were waiting to hear her story. She met their black-eyed stares briefly, then looked pleadingly at Daniel. Before she could speak, he made a remark which sent both Indians laughing again. Suddenly she felt as though she were being insulted somehow, and she lowered her reddening face. *How dare he embarrass me in front of these heathens!* She wrung her apron in both hands, wishing it were Daniel's neck.

"Eli noticed you have no pock marks," Daniel said.

Mary scowled at Daniel, her face still flushed with embarrassment. "Why should he care?"

Daniel's face sobered. "They mistrust most whites. Two years ago, they traded with a white man. He sold them blankets infected with the pox. Many of their people perished."

Mary glanced at the woolen blanket upon which she sat, suddenly concerned.

"Not these blankets," Daniel assured her. "These are clean."

Despite Daniel's assurances, Mary fidgeted uncomfortably on the blanket, praying she didn't contract some other horrible disease.

After the meal, Eli lit a pipe and two women entered the wigwam, looking at Mary with unabashed curiosity. Eli and Charles looked at Mary expectantly, and Daniel finally said, "They want you to go with them."

"Whatever for?" Mary demanded.

Daniel leaned in closer to her and said in a low whisper, "The women want to bathe you and give you fresh clothes. You....offend."

Mary gaped at him, again feeling her face redden. "*I offend?*" she hissed back, more insulted than she'd ever been in her life.

"Just go with them. If you refuse, you'll cause a scene."

Mary was speechless. Bathing was infrequent among the white settlers, and Mary wasn't about to bathe in the presence of strangers, much less heathens. Her eyes darted helplessly from Daniel to the waiting women. The older of the two gestured and scowled at Mary impatiently. Feeling she had no choice, she got up, almost tripping over her skirt. The younger of the two Indian women gave Mary what she surmised was a smile of encouragement. *I'm being led like a lamb to slaughter*, she thought darkly, resigning herself to whatever ill fate awaited her.

I had never known such a humiliation before or since, Daughter! I was led to a secluded bend in the river, where several Indian women and their little heathen children went about their morning tasks. They watched me with brazen interest while the older woman demanded I disrobe, grunting and pulling at my vestments. What could I do? What did it matter? Surely I would be killed or enslaved afterwards. I closed my eyes and wished I could be turned to a pillar of salt like Lot's wife as they stripped me, even of my coif! I kept my eyes closed the whole time as they scrubbed and manipulated my limbs in whatever pose they required. They immersed me, scrubbing my scalp vigorously. I was sure it was to ensure my poor scalp would make a handsome prize for one of their men. I wept during the entire ordeal, so fearful and ashamed was I. At one point the older woman seized my chin and shook my jaw open as if I were a horse. "Wàbòz Ikwe," she kept repeating. The others apparently agreed, and after she released my chin, I was led to the river bank and dried. At last my nakedness was covered by a doeskin tunic that exposed my pale calves. The garment was remarkably soft, adorned with pale wampum beads and porcupine quills. I was handed a beaded belt to tie around my waist. The younger woman proceeded to comb my tangled mass of hair, and plaited it in two neat braids. I wanted to request my coif, for I still felt naked without a covering for my head! I know not what they did with my old clothes, and after they slipped a pair of beaded moccasins on my feet, they seemed satisfied that I was fully attired.

Mary kept her eyes on the ground as the women led her through the village. She felt the eyes of every Indian scrutinizing her new appearance. They led her to where a bear hide was stretched fur-side down on the ground. The same two women Mary had seen before were still laboring over the skin with bone scrapers. Bits of fat still clung to the hide, and one of the women handed her a scraper.

And so begins my enslavement, Mary thought despairingly, kneeling on the smelly bear hide.

She spent the rest of the morning toiling over the hide, fighting back tears when the women would slap her hand in an apparent attempt to correct her mistakes. The late morning sun warmed her aching back and shoulders, and she wanted to cry out in frustration. Flies buzzed annoyingly over the bear skin and if she paused to swat them away, she was scolded. Her own shadow lay across the outstretched skin, sometimes mingling with the shadows of the other two women. And then a tall, lanky shadow appeared from behind her.

"You learn quick," Daniel remarked.

Hot and weary, Mary stopped and turned to squint up at him, shielding her eyes with one hand. His appearance had also transformed. He'd removed his ragged shirt and apparently bathed himself. He wore only fringed deerskin breeches and a tunic similar to hers but shorter. A large knife hung from his beaded belt, its polished antler hilt gleaming in the sun. Its sheath was covered in white and blue wampum beads. Next to it hung the small knife she'd freed him with. His beard was gone but he still wore his felt hat. Riff sat on his haunches at Daniel's side, panting softly. "Is this what you intended?" she rasped. "To make me a slave among these heathens?"

One of the women barked an order, pulling at her arm roughly.

"Don't stop working," Daniel said.

Mary threw the bone scraper in frustration and scrambled to her feet. The other women yelled in disapproval, and she ignored them, directing all her rage on Daniel. Clenching her fists, she stomped her moccasined foot with an unsatisfyingly soft *thump.*

"I'll not allow you or them to enslave me! I'd rather they kill me than endure this misery a second longer!"

"If you don't work, you don't eat," Daniel explained simply.

"Wàbòz Ikwe!" one of the women called impatiently, gesturing for Mary to get back to work.

"That's you," Daniel said.

Mary looked from the scowling woman to Daniel. "What?"

"Wàbòz Ikwe," he repeated, pointing at his own chipped from teeth, then at her overbite. "Rabbit Woman."

Chapter Eight

That first day among the savages seemed endless. When I unintentionally scraped a hole through the bearskin, I was directed to help dry fish, but I tripped, bringing the entire drying structure down, thus ruining the fish. Next, I was handed a crude digging stick and forced to dig up edible roots, but in my awkward attempts, I broke the implement. The head matron appeared so exasperated with me, she finally complained to Daniel, who lounged with the men playing some mindless game with dice. I was humiliated and exhausted, yet I still shed tears aplenty when Daniel finally came to speak with me on the old matron's behalf.

"Hurit says you're worthless," Daniel interpreted as the old woman ranted about Mary's ineptitude. The old woman narrowed her black eyes and scowled at Mary with blatant disgust.

Mary withered under the old woman's harsh gaze, but cried indignantly, "I'll not be made a slave!"

"You're not a slave," Daniel said, looking as if he was enjoying her misery. "You're a guest."

Her jaw dropped. "A *guest?* This is how they treat *a guest?*"

"Even guests are expected to earn their keep."

Mary scowled at Riff, ever present at his master's side. The big dog yawned. "That beast of yours does nothing to earn *his* keep."

Hurit continued to scowl, muttering something to Daniel. He

nodded and said to Mary, "What are you good at? Can you cook? Can you grind corn?"

Mary thought desperately. Returning Hurit's hateful gaze, she said stonily, "I can sew."

Daniel smiled, relaying this news to Hurit, who gave Mary a last scathing look before she disappeared into a nearby wigwam. The woman returned shortly with her arms full of tanned deer hides. She dropped the pile onto the ground next to what appeared to be a Christian cross formed from two small birch trees lashed together. Hurit gestured impatiently for Mary to join her, making sewing motions with her hands.

"Then you just may have found your salvation," Daniel said.

So I'm to be a seamstress for savages! Mary thought glumly, blowing a loose lock of hair off her sweaty face. For the hundredth time, she regretted helping Daniel escape, and cursed him under her breath.

Mary was given the task of sewing deer hide tunics, threading fine strands of sinew through bone needles and using the T-shaped stand as a dress form. She stabbed her blistered fingers, darkening the soft hides with bloodstains. When Hurit discovered that, she ripped the stained hides from Mary's hands, thrusting a thick leather thimble at her and giving her a fresh deer skin to sew.

While she labored at her task, Mary observed the residents of the Indian village with a growing sense of reluctant admiration. There were surprisingly few children, and the ones who acknowledged Mary did so shyly. Riff had planted himself next to her, resting his big head on his front paws. Suddenly he lifted his head, his ears cocked in interest. Mary looked up to see two little boys, perhaps five or six years old arguing just yards away from her. The larger boy pushed the smaller one, whose indignant wails caught the attention of both Charles and Daniel. Mary watched with interest as Charles questioned the boys. While the little one sniffled and wiped his nose on his bare arm, the older one pointed accusingly at the other. Charles knelt to the child's level and spoke softly to him, the morning sun blaring off the man's shaven head. The warrior's strong, commanding face softened as he laid a big hand on the older child's shoulders. Mary's mouth fell open as the older child nodded, a repentant look growing on his face. He said some words to his little companion, who smiled before accepting the other's hand. Mary looked on as the two boys ran off together, laughing.

Later, Mary asked Daniel what had transpired.

"Achak, the elder brother, accused Ahanu of losing his ball." Daniel explained. "Charles told him he saw the ball in amongst some dear hides in that wigwam yonder, and told Achak to apologize, for he should never strike his brother."

"If you ask me," Mary said, "Achak could have used a good paddling."

Daniel shook his head. "'Tis not their way. Striking a child is abhorrent to these people."

This concept was foreign to Mary. "Sparing the rod spoils the child."

"Charles would rather cut off his own arm before he beat a child."

Now Mary was thoroughly confused. The little boys had run off happily, and Charles' style of discipline appeared to have worked. "But," she stammered more to herself, "these people are savages…"

Daniel gave her a steady look. "Are they?"

He gestured to a pair of women conversing amicably as they ground corn. Two warriors walked past, their laughter like distant thunder. One young woman combed the thinning grey locks of an elderly lady. The scene was peaceful, and the entire village had a relaxed, content atmosphere.

Mary struggled to make sense of this form of child-rearing. Corporal punishment or the threat thereof, was a cornerstone of discipline in every family Mary knew. As she looked on in wonder, Charles walked by and flashed her a warm smile.

She bent her head over her sewing, wondering just who indeed were the true savages.

By noon, the men had assembled in communal circles, given bowls of samp and smoked venison to eat. Famished, Mary collapsed next to Daniel, waiting to be served. Seeing this, Hurit seized Mary's arm and pulled her roughly to her feet. Mary looked to Daniel helplessly who simply said, "The women serve the men first."

Grudgingly, Mary was forced to offer the men their portions. Only after that was she allowed to rejoin Daniel and partake of the meal herself. She tore into the strip of jerky, relishing its smoky saltiness. She gulped spring water from a gourd cup noisily before wiping her mouth on her sleeve. Feeling only slightly refreshed, she turned to Daniel and asked, "Are we to stay here?"

Daniel offered Riff a slab of venison, and the dog accepted it happily. "Nay. We'll depart on the morrow. This is merely a rest stop."

Mary snorted derisively. "A rest stop for whom? Surely not me!"

He chose to ignore her, increasing her aggravation. Wiping his hands on his fringed breeches, he untied her small knife from his belt and handed it to her. "You can have this back," he said. "I won this larger one while gaming."

Mary accepted her knife, suddenly wishing she could thrust it into his ribs. Instead, she secured it to her own belt, feeling only slightly better that this small possession had been returned to her. A soft, familiar tinkling caught Mary's ear and she looked up to see a young woman striding out of a nearby wigwam. Her hair had been shorn, just barely brushing her shoulders, whereas the other women's hair was long. Mary gasped when she recognized her velvet pouch swinging from the woman's slender waist.

"My physicks!" she cried, suddenly ashamed she hadn't given a thought to Lizzie all morning. She scrambled to her feet and approached the startled young woman. She seized the velvet pouch, pulling on it frantically. "Give them to me!"

The Indian woman screamed, alarming other women, who came to their friend's defense, yelling at Mary and pushing her away. At last Daniel, Charles and Eli rose and sauntered casually to the group of shouting women. The angry shouts only subsided after Eli raised a hand. Despite being surrounded by angry women, Mary turned to Daniel. “Tell them! Those are mine!”

Daniel complied, and Eli said something calmly. “I told him they are for your sick sister. He says they are no use to you now. Your sister is not here.”

“Daniel, *please!*” Mary screamed, tears suddenly pouring down her tired face. “They belong to *me!*”

Mary’s erratic behavior drew looks of concern from her audience. She ignored all but Daniel, ready to fall on her knees before him.

Daniel’s face reddened and he grabbed her arm. “Stop it! You are making a scene.”

“I want my physicks,” she demanded, sobbing. “If only to remind me of Lizzie.”

Daniel released her arm and exhaled deeply before pleading her case to Eli, who thought a moment before speaking to the terrified young woman Mary appeared to be attacking. The Indian woman had begun to cry too, and tears shimmered in her large brown eyes as she untied the pouch from her waist. She handed it to Eli, her delicate hand trembling. The velvet pouch swung by its cord in the old man’s hand, and he presented it to her stoically.

“Say *meegwetch*,” Daniel instructed in a low voice. “That means ‘thank you.’”

“I’ll not!” Mary snapped, hastily tying the pouch to her belt. “The Devil can take me before I thank these heathens for returning to me what is rightfully mine!”

Once I’d gained possession of my physicks, the day soured even further. Kezia dearest, may you never be exposed to such hateful glances as were cast my way after that horrid incident. Now even Hurit ignored me. She’d express something to Daniel, who seemed to begrudge being put in such an awkward position. I stood about, uncertain what to do, and that day dragged on endlessly. Towards sunset, I was so weary I nearly fell

asleep serving the men their sup, and was most grateful when we were allowed to rest in the wigwam of Charles and his family. The accommodations were cramped, and I lay awake pressed between the bark wall and Daniel. The dog lay at our feet, snoring. Bone-weary and still angry at him for allowing the savage Indian women to mistreat me so, I loathed lying beside him.

"Stop your fidgeting," Daniel hissed, lying on his back with his hat over his face. "You're disturbing everyone."

"How can I sleep, without a proper bed, crammed in like too many chicks in a nest?" She shifted her elbow, hitting it painfully on one of the wigwam's birch supports. "God's eyes!" she cursed, rubbing the sore elbow.

Daniel sat up, his hat tumbling from his face into his lap. His movement woke Riff, who lifted his shaggy head from his paws and yawned. Daniel pulled her up by one arm. "Get up. Get up and stay quiet."

She was too tired to resist, and allowed herself to be pulled to her feet. Riff got up also, tail wagging slowly as he followed them out of the wigwam, taking care not to step on any sleeping Indians.

Daniel dragged her out to the river bank, his hand still tight around her arm. When they came to a large limestone boulder, he ordered, "Sit."

She glared at him, but obeyed, just as Riff sat on his haunches next to her.

He's mastered me like he has this mutt of his, she thought scornfully.

Daniel sat next to her, leaning against the boulder with his long legs stretched towards the river. The still-full moon glowed like a pearl, sending a shimmer of moonlight trailing across the still water. The late evening air was heavy and fragrant, filled with the sounds of crickets and other night animals. Daniel regarded her with those intense green eyes of his and if she weren't so tired and frustrated, she might have felt a spark of the attraction she'd first felt towards him.

Instead, she continued to glare at him, resisting the heaviness of her eyelids.

"We'll not enter that wigwam again until you can lie still."

"Daniel," she whined, "I am exhausted. I *want* to sleep, but how can I when--"

He pulled her again by the arm until she found herself sitting in the V of his long legs. "Lie back."

Placing his hands on her aching shoulders, he massaged them with firm, rhythmic pressure until her muscles began to relax. She sighed at the pleasurable sensation as he pulled her back to recline against his hard chest. His arms wrapped comfortably around her waist and she sagged against him like a rag doll. She felt all her weariness melt away as if his body was absorbing it from hers. Riff came to lie beside them, pressing his warm furry body against their legs. Crickets chirped and stars hung in the sky, winking down at her. Her hands covered his, and she felt the T branded into his flesh. She remembered him stoically bearing the pain of that punishment, the blanching of his face the only sign he felt any discomfort. She traced the brand with her finger as feelings for him began to return.

"I'm sorry they did that to you."

"I've felt worse pain," he said in a low voice. "And I'm likely to feel still worse before I give up the ghost."

She couldn't comprehend a life of pain and misery, and when he flipped his palms upwards, her hands fell into them like nesting birds and her fingers interlaced with his. "It's times of strife and trial we must most rely on our faith in God."

He snorted derisively. "I've no faith in a God who allows evil things to happen to good people, such as Charles and his folk."

She cocked her head and peered up at his shadowed face. "You mean that business with the contaminated blankets?"

"Aye," he replied. "I've lived among these folks off and on many a time, and they are a far more honorable people than many of our kind, God's honest truth."

Mary frowned, digesting this information. She'd been taught to fear and avoid the godless savages, and had never heard anyone speak in their defense. "Daniel," she whispered, looking out at the wide expanse of river, "I'm afraid for us."

If he answered her, she never heard him. Almost before the last words left her lips, she'd fallen asleep.

The next morning, I awoke to find myself alone in the wigwam. Daniel must have carried me back inside, for I didn't remember returning. When Hurit discovered I was awake, she hustled me out of the wigwam and put me to work cleaning fish the young boys had caught that morning. I made a ghastly mess of the fish, and again the old bawd scolded me.

And so went my life among the Indians. My days were filled with back-breaking work, but the Indian women never complained, and accepted their lot in life with admirable grace. Each night, I collapsed on the wigwam floor in a sore and aching heap.

No one but Daniel's dog seemed to notice when on the third day, I slipped away to sit on the river bank, reclining against the rock Daniel had rested against. Riff appeared to be the only creature sympathetic to my plight, and he allowed me to scratch his head while I cried. The velvet pouch reminded me of sweet Lizzie, and was but bittersweet consolation. I fondled the pouch just to hear the soft, familiar tinkle of the vials, I was deep in my despair when Riff raised his head from my lap and glanced curiously upriver. Then from within his massive throat rumbled a most ominous growl.

Mary rose and shaded her eyes with her hand, trying to see what had attracted Riff's attention. A pair of canoes drifted steadily in the wide expanse of river. Two men occupied the largest of the two crafts, towing an empty one behind them. The one in the front held a musket casually in his arms while the man in the rear maneuvered the craft with a single oar. They wore wide-brimmed hats, and appeared to be white men. Three other forms moved about in the occupied canoe; as they grew closer Mary saw that they were bloodhounds. As they grew closer, she heard their long, howling barks. Still confused, she turned to Riff, but the dog was already making its way back to the Algonquin village.

They're searching for Daniel and me! The realization hit her like a splash of cold water, and she bolted after Riff as if she were being pursued by the devil himself.

Chapter Nine

With her heart struggling to escape her chest like a caged bird, Mary ran to the village. Riff had arrived ahead of her, barking excitedly. She found Daniel in the midst of a group of men, playing yet another game while the village women labored at their chores. "Daniel! Daniel, they're coming for us!"

Daniel and Charles were the first to rise to their feet, the game apparently forgotten. Daniel grabbed her shoulders as she panted, catching her breath. "Mary, what did you see?"

"Two men with three dogs," she reported, her chest heaving. "Oh, Daniel, I'm quite sure they're coming for us--"

"Corwin and Dounton," Daniel muttered the names like a curse. Even before Daniel had time to translate this news to the Indians, Charles and his warriors disappeared into nearby wigwams, returning with muskets and bows and arrows. Charles handed Daniel a musket, powder horn and shot bag. Releasing Mary's shoulders, he accepted the weaponry and demanded, "Show us where."

Riff led the way back to the river bank, crouching low as Daniel and the Indians positioned themselves behind trees, peering upriver. The approaching threat was closer now and Daniel motioned for her to go back to the village. Ignoring his silent order, Mary knelt behind the same limestone boulder she'd visited earlier. From her position she could see Daniel and Charles, crouched and still as stones. Mary held her breath as the two canoes drifted closer. Sweat trickled from her brow, stinging her eyes. She dared not even blink for fear of being detected. She could clearly see the two men now. The oarsman puffed casually on a pipe while his companion scoured the forest, cradling his musket. She could hear the men's voices, low and somber. The three hounds held their snouts aloft, sniffing the late afternoon air. A gentle breeze was blowing downriver, and Mary suspected the dogs hadn't picked up their scent yet because of that. As if to confirm her suspicions, she caught the smell of tobacco smoke from the oarsman's pipe.

Heavenly Father, Mary prayed silently, *shield us from our pursuers! If You deliver us, I'll—I'll become a papist and join a nunnery!*

She didn't know where this vow came from, but suddenly a safe, cloistered life held great appeal to her. Her father would disown her and Lizzie would never forgive her, but she decided that if she survived this ordeal, she would resign herself to such a life. Daniel's words from the night before echoed in her head. Surely times of great strife were when faith was most needed, she told herself. *I could make my way to Quebec, and start a new life--*

The canoes drifted past at an achingly slow pace and uncomfortably close to the shore. Not even birdsong was heard as Mary crouched behind the boulder. Daniel and Charles' warriors remained frozen until the canoes drifted past a bend in the river and out of sight. Several moments after their pursuers were well out of sight, Daniel and the Indians remained still. Even Riff lay motionless, still as a fallen log next to Daniel. At last, Charles whistled like a lark and Daniel and the others relaxed, rising to their feet and heading back towards the village. Mary rose from her hiding spot as Daniel approached, sure he would scold her for disobeying him. Instead he simply grabbed her arm and dragged her so quickly back to the village she almost tripped. She wanted to protest but his stern expression stifled her.

Once inside the village, Charles began shouting orders at the Indian women. They immediately stopped their chores, then ducked into their wigwams. Several returned with armfuls of provisions. Hurit herself thrust two woolen blankets into Mary's arms, her expression a mixture of urgency and concern that Mary would have found heartening if she'd had the presence of mind to analyze it. The other women handed her pouches of pemmican, venison and dried berries along with a sliver of flint. Mary was so frightened and confused she only stood there, accepting the offerings without question. She turned a panicked face to Daniel, who said, "We're leaving. They will be back, and I'll not bring their wrath on the good people of this village."

"Where will we go?" Mary finally croaked over the lump of fear in her throat. She felt Riff press his head against her thigh and heard him whine softly.

"We'll take the canoe down one of the tributaries as far as that will take us, then we'll continue East to New London. Should take us but a day or two." He headed towards the river bank, the musket, powder horn and shot bag slung across his shoulders. She struggled to catch up to him, hugging the provisions to her chest. When they returned to the river, some of the warriors had already untied Daniel's small canoe. Riff seemed to sense the seriousness of their plight, and bounded into Daniel's canoe without the gleeful enthusiasm he'd expressed the first night. It was early evening, and the sun was just beginning to dip below the trees. Daniel grabbed the provisions from her and tossed them into the canoe before helping her board the wooden vessel. Once Daniel was seated with the oar in his hands, two warriors shoved the little craft into the river. The rest of the village gathered on the river bank to watch the departure. Sitting in the canoe, she faced the assembled Indians. To her surprise, Hurit raised her hand in farewell, which brought a lump to Mary's throat. She was even more astonished to see the woman's concerned expression on her usually-scowling face. *Why, the old bawd's weeping!* Mary realized, tears smarting behind her own eyes as she returned the gesture.

They drifted in silence until the Indians were out of sight. Mary released her breath then she turned to Daniel, who began to paddle rhythmically as he'd done that first night.

"Why New London?" she finally asked after the Indians had retreated from sight.

"We'll find a ship bound for England and board."

"*England?*" she cried. "Why--"

"Because nobody is hunting us in England."

The prospect of crossing the ocean frightened her even more. If she survived the journey, it ensured she would never see Lizzie again.

She stared at the bundle of provisions at her feet and sobbed. *I have ruined my life,* she thought morosely. Her stomach felt sick and she wanted to retch.

The sun blazed orange through the trees as twilight fell. The moon, as round and white as a pearl, glared down at them like the All-Seeing Eye of God that adorned her father's pulpit back in Hereford. The late summer air was still now, the river smooth as glass. The only sounds Mary heard besides Daniel's slow, rhythmic paddling were the far-off cries of animals hidden in the woods. Daniel remained silent, his eyes scouring both sides of the river. He steered the canoe onto the first tributary they came to, veering in the direction of the disappearing sun. The tension was so maddening Mary wanted to scream in frustration. Finally she said in a quiet voice, "How do those men know you?"

"Corwin had me arrested, along with my mother, for witchcraft. The burly fellow with the pipe is Dounton, the jailer." Hatred hardened his features and iced his words, sending shivers down Mary's spine. "They're as cruel as if they'd been sired by Satan himself."

Mary's eyes widened. She'd heard of the witchcraft hysteria that had infected three Massachusetts counties the year before. "Tell me of your mother," she pressed, her own mother's face forming in her mind.

Instantly some of the hardness in his face dissolved. "A better woman you'd never find."

"Did she…did she hang?"

"Nay. Providence intervened, and she avoided Dounton's noose by a sheer miracle."

Mary smiled, relieved. "Then she lives?"

His eyes softened, but his words were clipped with sorrow and regret. "Aye. She lives, but with a broken heart."

"What was her name?"

His face softened somewhat. "Her name was Rebecca."

She wanted to ask more, but Daniel pointed with his chin at the left river bank. Mary glanced into the moonlit woods as several dark figures skulked in and out of the shadows. Riff cocked his ears and growled softly. She turned to Daniel fearfully.

"Wolves," he said.

The narrow tributary grew shallow, moss-covered rocks breaking the surface like a chain of tiny islands. Daniel leaped out of the canoe into knee-deep water, Riff bounding after him. Mary loathed the prospect of getting her feet wet again, and waited until Daniel pulled the craft up onto the rocky bank. Like a gentleman, he extended his hand and helped her out. Her foot slipped on a mossy rock, but his steadying hand saved her. Wordlessly they pulled the canoe deeper into the woods. Daniel removed the blankets and provisions from the canoe and set them on the ground. He directed her with monosyllabic commands as together they turned the canoe onto its side, propping it up with the single oar and a birch sapling. After Mary smoothed the blankets on the ground, they'd formed a crude shelter.

"Look for the smallest, driest twigs, and some grass," he said. "I'll build us a fire."

Fortunately, the late summer forest floor was littered with just the sticks Daniel needed. She kept close to both Daniel and Riff as she stooped to gather the tinder. *Surely this dog will alert us to any danger,* she assured herself, and when Riff regarded her with a lazy yawn, she relaxed.

Daniel retrieved the sliver of flint from the bundle of provisions. He struck it against his knife four times before a smattering of sparks ignited the tinder. He blew on the young embers gently, and then seated himself on the blanket next to Mary while the smokeless little fire burned merrily. Riff seated himself on Daniel's other side and rested his snout on his paws.

Her hands fondled the little pouch at her waist, and the short-haired Indian woman's sad, pretty face came to mind.

"The Indian maid who had my physicks, " she asked suddenly. "Why was her hair bobbed thus?"

"That was Alawa," he said. "Charles' sister. Her husband was killed not long ago, and her shorn hair is a sign of mourning."

She suddenly felt compassion for the young woman, and regretted being so rude to her. Hurit's disapproving face floated in her mind, conjuring mixed feelings. It was true the Indian women were demanding, but they hadn't been abusive. Still holding the pouch, her thoughts turned to Lizzie. She remembered carelessly pouring the measure of tincture into the rum jug, and fresh tears of remorse seeped from her eyes. *Forgive me, Jailer Dirby,* she prayed. The old man had always been kind to her and Lizzie, and she had killed him. She stared sadly into the fire, entranced by the dancing flames. "I'm a murderess," she said in a dead, flat voice.

Daniel sat with his forearms resting on his knees, tossing small sticks into the fire at regular intervals. The T on his hand glared conspicuously in the moonlight. "You didn't murder Dirby. 'Twas an accident."

"Have you ever killed anyone?"

When he didn't immediately answer, she tore her eyes from the mesmerizing fire and gasped at the coldness in his eyes. "Killed," he conceded icily. "But not murdered."

His admission chilled her as if she'd been doused with a bucket of river water. She immediately regretted her inquiry, and drew her knees up to her chin. Despite the warmth of the fire, her skin crawled with icy fear.

"Don't look so fearful of me," he growled, snapping a long twig in half before tossing it into the flames. "I won't hurt you."

She realized she was trembling, and hugged her folded legs against her chest. Could she believe him? Could she trust him? She really knew nothing about him. She thought of the first night among the Indians, how comfortably she'd lain against him as reclined against the rock. So many conflicting emotions swirled for dominance her head began to throb. Gazing into the fire, her mind conjured up images of Lizzie, and her vision blurred with unshed tears. Suddenly, the tension was too much and she dissolved into loud, gulping sobs.

"Because of me, a man is dead," she lamented, cradling her face in her hands. "And I will never see Lizzie nor my father again."

She heard him remove his tunic then shift position on the blanket, and drape an arm over her shoulders. She leaned helplessly against his bare chest, ashamed to show such weakness in front of him. He rocked her gently, allowing her to grieve for her past life. When her tears were spent, he lifted her face to his, and she drew in a sharp breath. His eyes smoldered like embers and before she could register what was happening, his mouth was on hers. Her arms went instinctively around his shoulders as he pushed her onto the blanket, and again she felt as if she were falling into a fathomless abyss.

Her hands explored his scar-riddled back, and it occurred to her he must have been flogged at one point. For some reason, this brought to mind Noah Parker's scowling, doughy face. For a moment she imagined it was Noah she was lying with, but her stomach clenched in revulsion. She shook the offending image from her mind and returned Daniel's kiss fervently.

Instead of whispering sweet endearments, Daniel grunted coarse and ugly words into her ear, causing her to flush hot with shame. His entry was painful and she cried out softly. She'd never been with a man before, and had nothing with which to compare this experience. *I am a murderess, a fugitive and a fornicator,* she realized. *I am a fallen woman and beyond redemption. Even a nunnery wouldn't accept me now.*

Afterwards, he rolled off her. She stared at his scarred back, fresh tears dampening her eyes. She felt sore inside. With their intermingled scent in her nostrils, she lay there, listening to the sounds of the forest. A falling star zipped fleetingly across the night sky, and Mary hugged herself against a new chill.

I am like that star, she thought despairingly. *Helpless, fallen and ruined.*

Beside her, Daniel snored, oblivious to her anguish.

Chapter Ten

She awoke the next morning to find herself alone in the little shelter. For a moment she felt disoriented, then she flushed at the memory of the events the night before. Her mouth was dry and she couldn't recall the last time she'd eaten anything as her stomach complained loudly.

The fire had died down to mere embers and the forest was filled with birdsong. A large spider web bejeweled with dew drops glittered in the sunlight between two young saplings. She sat up, wrapping one of the blankets around her shoulders.

"Daniel?" she called tentatively, her voice sounding hoarse and foreign to her own ears. When all she heard were more birdsong, she got to her feet and inspected their camp. The provisions were just as they'd left them, but the musket, shot bag and powder horn were missing.

Surely he's not abandoned me, she assured herself. *He'd have taken the provisions if he had. Mayhap he's gone to fetch us breakfast,* she told herself.

Rubbing her eyes, she walked to the tributary, her mocassined feet soundless on the dewy forest floor. She grasped low-hanging tree limbs to steady herself as she negotiated the moss-covered rocks. Mary glanced both upstream and down, but only saw a raccoon look up from the opposite shore before scurrying into the woods. She knelt carefully, cupped her hands and lowered them into the cool water. She drank, her parched throat reveling in the relief. Then she splashed her face with more water, hoping to rouse herself to wakefulness. Still kneeling on the rocks, she listened again for any sound of Daniel, or even Riff. A doe and two fawns dipped their graceful heads into the tributary's depths several yards away, and Mary smiled. She imagined the fawns were sisters, and that brought Lizzie to mind. Absently she reached for the velvet pouch to comfort herself, but it was missing.

Shocked, she glanced at her waist. The pouch was gone from her belt, and she got up hastily, slipping on the field of rocks. Her ankle twisted painfully as she scoured the forest floor, retracing her steps to the upturned canoe. Frantically, she shook out the blankets and checked behind the bundle of provisions. Her panic rose when she couldn't find the velvet pouch at the campsite.

My only link to Lizzie! She screamed silently, a fresh batch of hot tears scalding her eyes. *Oh, Little One, forgive me! I miss you so!*

Convinced the pouch was lost forever, she collapsed onto the blanket. With her ankle throbbing, she dropped her head into her hands and wept. She was so lost in her sorrow and heartache she didn't hear Daniel's approach and she startled when Riff nudged her with his wet snout. She looked up to find Daniel holding three dead rabbits by their ears in one hand, the musket in the other.

"Clean these," he said, tossing the small carcasses at her feet. "Don't let that fire die. We'll eat and then move on."

She looked up at him, her cheeks awash with tears. "I've lost my physicks," she sniffed.

He scowled slightly. "When?"

"I don't know," she sobbed, drawing her feet away from the dead rabbits whose glassy eyes seemed to follow her. "I can't find them anywhere."

Daniel seemed concerned, but not for her personal loss. He unsheathed his large knife and handed it to her. "Get to work on these rabbits; I'll get more wood for the fire."

Wiping her nose on her arm, she glared at him. "Do you not care I've lost my only connection to Lizzie?"

"I care more that someone might come across that pouch and use it to find us," he replied. "Mayhap you lost it last night while we gathered wood. I'll look for it." He looked pointedly at the rabbits. "Get them cleaned quickly."

You dark-hearted lout! She wanted to scream. *Have you no sentimentality at all?* She continued to glare at his retreating back before she seized the first rabbit by its ears and plunged the knife into its soft underbelly with impotent rage.

Her butchering was clumsy and messy. She made a mess of the soft grey pelts, and the rabbits' blood stained the entire front of her tunic. Her gorge rose as she pulled out the greasy entrails and flung them aside for Riff to devour. She hadn't finished the first rabbit before Daniel returned with an armful of dry sticks. When he saw the mess she was making of the rabbits, he took the knife from her and said, "You tend the fire. I'll butcher."

Relieved, Mary handed him the knife and they switched places. She wanted to ask if he'd found the velvet pouch, but it was obvious he hadn't. She fed the fire with one slender twig at a time while he butchered the rabbits with an impressive efficiency. When she couldn't stand the silence anymore, she demanded, "Speak to me or I'll go mad!"

He lobbed off the last rabbit's head, then glanced at her casually. "What now, pray?"

While he was collecting firewood, so many angry words had bubbled in her throat. Now that she had his attention, she hesitated, gathering her thoughts so that she'd speak coherently. "Last night," she said finally. "I want to talk about that."

One corner of his mouth twitched as he gutted the last rabbit. "So talk."

His coolness was infuriating and she exhaled in exasperation. "Last night, when--"

His green eyes never left as he labored over the rabbit. When he didn't answer, she felt angry and ashamed. Of course it wasn't love for him. He'd taken advantage of her, and that was all it was to him. Hurt, she flushed and stared at her bloodstained hands.

"Last night was what it was," he said simply. Then as if it just occurred to him to ask, he said, "how fare you?"

He hadn't answered her question, and her outrage still simmered. "I am hurt," she confessed. "I thought…I thought 'twould be different."

Daniel placed two Y-shaped sticks at opposite points of their fire and thrust the three rabbit carcasses onto them. Riff was still devouring the entrails, his black snout stained with blood. As Daniel slowly rotated the rabbits over the fire, a delightful scent rose in the air, making Mary's stomach growl. Finally, Daniel said, "You didn't tell me to stop."

This surprised her. She looked from the roasting rabbits to him. "If I had, would you have stopped, truly?"

"I don't force women," Daniel said, finally meeting her eyes. He looked sincere, and she wanted to believe him. This news doused her outrage slightly.

"But do you have feelings for me?" She pressed.

He raised the spit off its supports and inspected the seared meat before returning it to the flames. Several moments passed in silence. It drove her mad that he wouldn't answer her questions immediately. She was going to insist he answer when he reached for a length of doeskin. Draping it over one of the roasted rabbits, he pulled it off the spit. He handed it to her, and she held the warm, delicious-smelling meat in both hands.

"That one's done," he said.

She ate ravenously, resigned to her fate. The only one to blame for her predicament was herself. After they ate, Daniel rose to bundle the provisions while Riff gnawed contentedly on rabbit bones. He extended a hand to help her up, and she winced when she put pressure on the twisted ankle. He scowled with concern. "What ails you?"

"I twisted my ankle at the stream," she replied.

"Sit down," he said, and she returned to the blanket. He sat cross-legged in front of her, and gestured for her to offer him her injured ankle. She presented it to him and removed her moccasin. His hands on her bare foot sent those annoyingly thrilling sensations up her leg as he inspected the ankle, gently rotating her foot. She winced when he turned her foot inward, and he returned the foot to its original position. His hands were rough but his touch was gentle, confusing and frustrating her even more. She caught herself sighing with pleasure as he rubbed her injured foot. He flashed her an easy smile, sending her heart racing again. Finally she couldn't stand it.

"Do you feel nothing for me?" she demanded at last.

His steady gaze held hers. "I'm indebted to you for helping me escape," he said.

But he won't say he loves me, she thought, her bottom lip dipping into an indignant pout.

He continued to massage her foot. "If I didn't care for you, I would have left you to the lions in Hereford."

Some of her frustration ebbed, and her heart lightened. So he *did* have feelings for her! But then she remembered the danger they still faced, and she turned somber. "Daniel, what will become of us?"

He lifted her foot to his mouth and kissed the top of it so lightly it sent a thrill up her spine. "Only Providence knows," he replied.

He bound her injured ankle in strips of deer hide before they broke camp. It was a shame to part with the canoe, but there was no way they could carry it overland through the dense forest to the next body of water. He fashioned a walking stick for her from one of the birch saplings, then slung the pack of provisions on his back. They walked in comfortable silence. She felt better knowing he at least had feelings for her, and as they negotiated the rough terrain, her thoughts raced to the coming night. Would he take her again? Surely it would be better, now that she knew more what to expect. She smiled and flushed slightly as she followed him, Riff trotting faithfully alongside his master. Her hair was still plaited into the tight braids the Indian woman had made the morning before, and they swung freely with every step. Before her, Daniel's buckskin breeches clung to his legs and buttocks in a way that made her anticipate the coming night.

"How far might we travel in one day?" she asked, stumbling over a tree root behind him.

"I'm hoping to reach New London in a fortnight at the very longest," he replied, offering her a supportive hand. "We could travel a good fifteen miles a day, longer once your ankle heals."

Her hand slipped into his, and it felt like the two halves of a broken plate fitting together. They'd been walking all morning, and had entered a sun-splashed clearing. "We can stop here if you need to rest," he said, his eyes softer than she'd ever seen them.

She accepted this offer and they rolled out the blankets. He fashioned a makeshift tent with skins and straight-limbed saplings. A mere trickle of a brook babbled pleasantly and Mary sat on a rock, scratching Riff's shaggy head. Daniel stood at the edge of the water, a sharpened stick poised over a shimmering trout that seemed to be resting in the shallow stream. She held her breath until he plunged the spear into the water, and she rejoiced when he extracted the impaled fish.

He caught two more, and they supplemented this meal with mushrooms and wild berries. Fat, grey-bottomed clouds inched across the sky, and a warm breeze disturbed the nearby foliage. After they ate, he hung a possessive arm around her. She traced the T on his hand with a finger, then brought it to her lips and kissed it. Daniel looked at her again with those smoldering eyes. He eased her down on the blanket, and said in a low voice, "If you don't want this, tell me now." She flushed, nodding her assent, and they made love again. This time, she refused to entertain any thoughts of shame, and allowed herself to enjoy the experience. Her senses reveled in the scent and feel of him. And this time when she closed her eyes, the only face she saw was Daniel's. Later, she sighed, resting her head on his shoulder and burying her hand in his chest hair. She marveled at how well their bodies fit together. Despite their precarious situation, she felt safe with him. He stroked her arm as they lay together. *This is how it is to lie with a man*, she thought. And this time, she had no regrets.

For the next four days, they traveled southward, living on wild berries and whatever animals that fell to Daniel's snares. Each night she grew more accustomed to lying with Daniel, and she felt wonderfully safe and loved. He told her about his time in the Salem dungeon as she lay in his arms. She couldn't imagine the deplorable conditions he described, and wondered how anyone could survive such an ordeal.

"You displayed such courage to have endured," she breathed, her head resting on his shoulder.

"Nay," Daniel contradicted in a low voice, stroking her arm. "Not anywhere near the courage my mother demonstrated."

"Surely such mistreatment took its toll on her."

"She lost her toes to frostbite. That I know for certain," Daniel conceded softly. "Hinders her so that she walks with a cane. What it did to her soul, I can only imagine."

Mary felt his arm tighten around her shoulders and she shivered, thinking what a remarkably strong woman Rebecca Eames must have been. Her own mother had been more delicate, like Lizzie, and didn't endure hardships well. Mary admired the woman Daniel described, and fell asleep dreaming of a woman shivering in a cold and filthy dungeon.

The next morning, they broke camp and continued on their way. Mary was surprised they hadn't come across any white settlements, or Indians, for that matter. Mary commented on this as they negotiated a narrow path that meandered through a patch of forest so dense the sunlight barely penetrated the leafy canopy.

"We're avoiding any settlements," he explained, pushing back some low shrubs so she could pass by them easier. "As for Indians, they're everywhere."

She shivered in the cool, deep shade, glancing about warily. "They are?" she whispered.

"Aye. Who do you think made these paths we've been following?"

She hadn't considered that, and looked down to discover that they were indeed following a well-worn path. "What happens if they attack?"

"If we don't disturb them, they'll likely let us pass as they've been doing."

She stopped, certain she misheard him. He paused ahead of her, his jaw covered in two days of spiny stubble. Riff stopped too, and looked at her with patient brown eyes. Daniel took her hand in his and said, "Indians have been watching ever since we began this journey. Riff would let us know if any are about that mean us harm. Likely they'll leave us be."

She caressed the T on his hand, repeating the word "*likely*" to herself. She glanced up at him with trembling lips, wanting to believe they would continue to travel unmolested. She wanted him to hold her, but she knew they had to keep traveling. "Daniel, I'm so afraid for us."

His eyes softened in the way that made her heart dance. He seemed so strong and fearless. She remembered how he didn't make a sound when the brand seared the T into his flesh. He cupped her face in his hands and gave her a slow, deep kiss. For a moment her fears dissolved. When they parted, he flicked tears off her cheeks with his thumbs and smiled at her reassuringly. "Do you trust me?"

So far, he hadn't harmed her, and he certainly could do whatever he wanted with her in the wilderness. *He's surely committed crimes and sins aplenty*, she thought, *and has deceived others in sundry ways*. But her heart spoke with the strongest conviction, and she nodded. "Aye," she said. "I trust you."

Chapter Eleven

After the dense shade of the forest, they came upon a flat marshland, replete with cattails, reeds and willows. A variety of waterfowl glided across the algae-coated water and a pair of beavers glanced briefly at Mary and Daniel from their large domed dam. When Riff let out an excited yip, they plunged quickly in the water, flapping their wide, flat tails.

Mary was constantly shooing mosquitos from her face, but they still managed to bite wherever they could, leaving small, itchy welts. She'd suffered several minor scratches on her arms and legs, and they began to itch. The sun was descending ahead of them and she was overtaken by weariness.

"Daniel," she begged, "Might we stop for the night? I need to rest."

He turned to face her. "We've made good distance today. How fares your ankle?"

"The ankle's fine," she said, her eyelids feeling heavy. "But I fear I'll fall asleep where I stand."

Daniel frowned and laid a hand across her forehead. She knew he wouldn't want to make camp until evening, but her legs had grown heavy and she felt like she could sleep soundly for twenty years. He regarded her with concern, then removed the pack of provisions from his back. "You have a fever. We'll make camp then and start afresh in the morning."

She nodded gratefully and leaned against a willow tree while he smoothed out the blankets and draped hides over some tall rushes. She collapsed on the blankets while he built a fire, but she couldn't seem to get warm. Daniel cocooned her in both blankets, lying on top of her as she shivered. Even Riff's warm body pressed against her back did nothing to relieve her chills. Her muscles ached and she felt feverish. When she closed her eyes, large black spiders crept toward her. Upon opening them, the spiders sprang away into nothingness. At one point she saw Lizzie standing over her, pointing an accusing finger at her.

"You abandoned me, Sister," Lizzie said in the vision. *"You abandoned me for a murdering thief!"*

"Lizzie!" Mary cried out, yearning to embrace her sister's image, but it faded, and she wept mournfully. "Lizzie, forgive me!"

She was vaguely aware of Daniel lying over her, rubbing her legs and arms, whispering softly in her ear. She stared at the fire as twilight set in, the flames blurry in her vision. A layer of fog obscured the swamp, and giant snakes slithered towards her. She screamed and closed her eyes, but the snakes remained.

"Don't let them bite me!"

"I won't, my love," he promised, stroking her hair.

She faded in and out of consciousness, losing awareness of her surroundings. At one point she heard the church bell. She attempted to sit up, but Daniel held her down.

"Let me up!" she demanded weakly. "I need to fix Lizzie's physick before Father begins his sermon!"

"'Tis already done," he whispered. "I saw to it."

"But you don't know the dosage!" she protested, squirming beneath the sweat-soaked blankets. "It must be precise--"

"You showed me how to measure it, remember?" he said gently.

Her fevered mind considered this. She didn't remember showing him how to properly measure and administer the medicine, but she was too weary to argue. Her foggy mind seemed to recall that she may have shown Noah the proper dosage once. She swallowed painfully and tried to smile. She withdrew a hand from the beneath the blankets and embraced his.

"Thank you, Noah."

Mary languished in a feverish stupor for two more days, barely aware of her own existence. The fever finally broke, leaving her feeling as weak as a kitten. She opened her bleary eyes to find Daniel hunkered over the bundle of provisions. He had kicked sand over the fire to extinguish it, and not one ember remained. Riff was by his side, and the dog looked at her and greeted her with a soft yip. It appeared to be morning, but she couldn't be sure. She stretched her arm out towards him, reaching for his hand, but he ignored her. Confused and slightly hurt, she attempted to sit up. She propped herself on her elbows, but a wave of dizziness overcame her and she fell back.

"Daniel," she croaked in a feeble voice.

"We lost three days due to your illness," he said flatly. "If you didn't wake this day, I was going to leave you."

His tone deepened her confusion. Surely he wasn't blaming her for contracting an illness? If she wasn't so weak, she would have cried. "Daniel," she tried again to reach out to him. "Why would you say something so hurtful?"

At last he looked at her, his eyes as cold and green as moss. She would have cringed if she'd had the strength. "I should have left you in Hereford."

Stricken, she didn't know what to make of his cruel words. "Daniel, why--"

"Shh!"

Riff cocked his ears and rose on his haunches, growling. She was going to ask what was wrong when he clamped a hand over her mouth. Her eyes widened as she heard the faint but distinct howling barks of multiple hunting dogs.

"If you ever truly trusted me," he whispered in a low voice, "you need to trust me now."

Thoroughly confused, she gasped feebly as he gathered her into his arms. She felt as limp as a rag doll. To Riff, Daniel commanded firmly, "Stay."

He waded into the swamp until he was waist-deep and only her knees and torso remained above the smelly green water. *He's going to drown me!* Her weakened mind screamed, and she tried to struggle but lacked the strength.

"Stop it," he ordered urgently. "Take a deep breath."

Before she knew it, he'd plunged them both into the stagnant water. They stayed immersed for a painfully long time as he moved quickly through the murkiness. Her lungs held insufficient oxygen, and she swallowed nasty water. She had no strength to resist him, and was about to lose consciousness when her head broke the surface. She gasped and sputtered, and found herself in a cave-like structure made of bark, twigs and mud. A flat shelf projected around almost half of the little cave, and it smelled strongly of musk. Daniel's head popped up next to her. He set her down, and her feet touched the swamp's sandy bottom. The water came up to her ribs, and Daniel planted her arms firmly on the earthen ledge.

"We're inside the beaver dam," he told her. "Stay quiet and wait until I come for you."

The barking sounded closer now. "Don't leave me!" she pleaded, reaching for him.

In the darkness of the beaver dam, she couldn't see anything, but she felt his hands cup her face, and he kissed her hard. Both her mind and heart were still confused, but his kiss retained its magic, and she wished she had the strength to embrace him. Before she could react, he dove back into the water, leaving her clinging to the muddy shelf, shivering chest-high in swamp water. Alone and terrified, she dropped her head on her folded arms and wept.

She strained to listen as the barking grew even closer. The report of musket fire shattered the air, and she jumped. Shivering from both fear and cold, she heard angry voices over the snarling and howling of dogs.

Dear God, deliver us! she prayed silently. She imagined Daniel's face in her mind, the rakish grin and cool, steady gaze of his green eyes. She held the image firmly in her mind, willing him to be safe. A dog yelped in pain, and she flinched, hoping it wasn't Riff.

More sounds of struggle ensued, and when she couldn't bear to hear it anymore, she clapped her hands over her ears and squeezed her eyes shut. *Keep Daniel safe. Keep Daniel safe,* she prayed silently.

She'd sealed off both sight and sound, but suddenly she detected smoke. Alarmed, she heard a crackling above her. Parts of the sturdy beaver dam began to give way, dropping down on her.

They've set the dam on fire! She realized. *I'll either drown or be burned alive!*

"Help!" she cried out, her voice echoing in the cavernous chamber. "God have mercy!"

She heard shouts directly above her, and what sounded like the dam being struck multiple times. The roof finally fell through, exposing the cloudless morning sky. Mud and dirt showered down on her, and she coughed, wiping grit from her eyes. She squinted upwards to see two men peering down at her. One puffed on a pipe as he regarded her with serpent-like eyes.

"Get her, Will," the other man said, a musket resting on his shoulder.

Exhaustion, fear and weakness enveloped her and as the barrel-chested man knelt to extract her from the ruined dam. Before his hands seized her shoulders, she collapsed into a dead faint.

Chapter Twelve

"She could pass for a heathen squaw easy," a gruff voice was saying when Mary finally came to. She smelled tobacco smoke and opened her eyes. She was being transported somehow, and she slowly became aware she was straddling a horse. A strong arm with a hairy-knuckled hand was clamped around her waist. To her horror, she discovered she'd been wrapped in one of the woolen blankets, but underneath she was naked. Reclining against her captor, she cringed in revulsion when she felt something hard press against her buttocks. The bowl of his pipe peered over her shoulder and blue smoke wafted into her face. She coughed, and heard him chuckle.

"She's awake, Corwin," he said to his companion, who was riding ahead of them on another horse. Three reddish brown bloodhounds trotted beside the horses, their long ears swaying to and fro.

"We'll be along the river soon," Corwin replied. "We'll snag us another canoe and be back in Hereford in less than two days."

Dounton's beefy hand migrated from her waist to her breast and squeezed it. Outrage surged within her, but she was too weak to protest and could only whimper pathetically. He laughed, billowing smoke-tainted foul breath over her shoulder.

"We'll have you back to your family in Hereford before you know it, Miss Mary," Corwin called over his shoulder. "My nephew will be pleased to have his betrothed returned to him."

She remembered Corwin was Noah's uncle, and she wondered what Noah told him. *Did Noah tell him I helped Daniel escape? Where is Daniel?* Her mind cried. Her mouth felt dry as dust and she couldn't remember the last time she'd eaten. She caught herself before she begged for water. I'll die of thirst before I beg anything of them, Mary vowed.

"What have you done with Daniel?" she was finally able to ask, her voice faint and rasping.

Dounton released a sinister laugh that chilled her heart. "Behind us on the litter. Don't worry, girlie. He'll get what's coming to him."

Daniel! She yearned to see him and struggled feebly against Dounton's broad chest, trying to catch a view of him. "Is he—does he live?"

Dounton chortled. "He lives. There's more bounty on a live fugitive than a dead one. 'Tis why we relieved you of your wet clothes. Can't have you dying on us."

She squirmed in agony, knowing that Daniel was so near and yet she couldn't embrace him. She didn't even have the strength to call out to him. She slumped against Dounton, aching to at least hear Daniel's voice.

They rode on until midday. At last they made camp along a river bank. The broad, meandering ribbon of water reminded her of the Great River, but surely they hadn't reached it that soon? Her sense of time was warped and she felt like she'd been straddling this horse and inhaling Dounton's foul breath for an eternity.

When they stopped, Dounton roughly deposited her into Corwin's waiting arms. The blanket fell away, exposing her bare legs. She'd never straddled a horse before, and her stiff, aching legs felt bowed. Corwin placed her in the shade of a locust tree and the three bloodhounds rested nearby, regarding her with their sad, drooping eyes. Finally she caught sight of Daniel, bound tightly and reclining on a litter. He'd been stripped of his tunic and his bloodied face looked sunburned. His hands had been bound behind his back and his legs were also tied tightly together. Both Corwin and Dounton half-dragged, half-carried him to the locust tree and threw him down next to her. Daniel appeared to be unconscious but when his body hit the ground, he released a dull moan. Corwin had slung her tunic, belt and moccasins over his shoulder. She covered herself as best she could with the blanket, sickened at the knowledge these men had seen her naked.

Corwin carelessly tossed the articles of clothing on the ground beside her. "These are dry now."

She withdrew one bare arm to pull the garments under the blanket with her. Her captors sniggered in amusement at her awkward attempt to dress herself while still concealing her nudity from beneath the blanket. Her face blazed with shame as she adjusted the tunic and tied the belt around her waist. As best she could, she pushed her personal outrage aside and crept closer to Daniel, who lay on his back, his eyes closed.

"Daniel, wake up," she begged, fat tears splashing onto his bruised face. "My darling--"

Dounton and Corwin lifted their brows. "*Darling?*" Corwin echoed nastily. "Fie, Miss Mary! How will you explain that to my nephew?"

She didn't care. At least Daniel was alive and with her. She kissed his split lip and swollen eyes. To her relief, his eyes fluttered open. They regarded her with somber sorrow. Dounton approached her with a gourd canteen. "Eames is awake," he announced to Corwin, then he kicked Daniel in the ribs. Daniel grunted and Mary cried out. She leaned forward to embrace Daniel, but Dounton grabbed her arm and pulled her up into a sitting position. "Drink some water," he said, thrusting the gourd to her mouth. "Can't have you perish afore we get to Hereford."

She wanted to resist, but the moment the cool water touched her lips, she drank greedily. She rejoiced as her parched throat was soothed, but after a few gulps, she pushed the gourd away. "Pray, give Daniel some."

Dounton snorted derisively. "Help yourself, "he said placing the gourd in her bound hands. "I'll be damned if I quench that bastard's thirst."

She took the gourd awkwardly and crept closer to Daniel. With effort, she maneuvered his head into her lap. "Daniel, take a drink."

She held the canteen at a clumsy angle and much of the water fell on his chest. Finally he was able to swallow a few mouthfuls, his eyes again filled with remorse. "Forgive me, Mary," he croaked.

Her heart both sang and ached at the sound of his voice. She bent down and kissed him, wishing they could disappear again into the wilderness together, never to be discovered.

Corwin chuckled at the tender scene. Hoisting his musket to his shoulder, he said to Corwin, "The girl's skin and bones. Hand her some of this cornbread while I scare us up some victuals." He tossed a drawstring pouch at Dounton, who caught it with one hand and removed a hard square of cornbread from it. He held out the crumbly yellow bread, and her stomach growled. Pushing aside her own hunger, she said firmly, "I'll do whatever you ask of me if you'll but set him upright and allow me to feed him."

Dounton lifted a brow and replaced the cornbread in the pouch. He got to his feet and walked to where the horses had been tethered. Returning with another length of rope, he grabbed Daniel by the arm and dragged him to the locust tree. She locked eyes with Daniel as he was bound securely to the tree trunk. Once Dounton was satisfied with his knots, he again produced the square of cornbread. Breaking it in half, he handed it to her. "That's all he gets."

Bittersweet memories of feeding him in the jail cell engulfed her, and she held his gaze as he accepted the morsel of cornbread. His lips on her fingers delivered the same thrilling sensation they did that first night, and she smiled sadly. When he had eaten the last crumb, Dounton extracted the remaining half. He held it out to her but when she reached for it, he withdrew it. "I want Eames to watch you eat from my hand."

Daniel squirmed in frustration against the ropes. Hatred streamed from his eyes like sunbeams directed at Dounton. "Don't you touch her, Dounton," Daniel growled. "She's a grown woman, not a girl child like you fancy."

Dounton sneered and drove a fist into Daniel's already-beaten face. Mary shrieked at the impact, and shrunk back in horror when Dounton turned his snakelike eyes on her. "Watch," he said to Daniel.

She shuddered in revulsion, but again her pride left her as she succumbed to her hunger, devouring the bread like a starved dog. It was the first solid food she'd had in days, and she tried to avoid touching his hand with her mouth. After the last crumb was gone, he grasped her chin and pried her mouth open. He thrust a dirty finger in her mouth, leering at her as her tongue involuntarily explored it. Mary's grey eyes glared at him in outrage and her face burned with shame. She tried to bite down hard, but even her jaw was too tired to cause much injury, and he pulled his thumb out quickly, slapping her face.

"None of that, wench." Dounton snarled as she recovered from the forceful slap. She'd never been struck before, and she tasted blood. *Don't cry in front of them,* she ordered herself, but to deepen her shame, tears welled up and she whimpered.

"Dounton," Daniel said in a hard voice, "I promised in Salem I'd strangle you one day with my bare hands. Now I swear it."

Dounton expelled an unimpressed snort and Mary scrambled to Daniel's side, inspecting his freshly bloodied face.

"Daniel," she whispered, stroking his cheek as tenderly as she could. "Tell me what to do!"

Both his eyes were bruised and swelling shut. "You do what you need to survive," he said.

Even when his face was so horribly battered, his look made her feel like the most beautiful and loved woman in the world. Before she could reply, a musket discharged, nearly jolting her heart out of her chest. She looked to see Corwin emerge from the woods, grasping a wild turkey by its scaly legs.

She remained by Daniel's side while Corwin prepared the turkey. The succulent smell as it roasted over the spit drove her mad with hunger. When their captors had their fill, Dounton returned with the water gourd and a perfectly roasted slab of turkey breast. He held the meat out to her tantalizingly; clearly enjoy seeing her drool in anticipation.

"Miss Mary, before I let you feed Eames, I'm going to feed you one strip of this at a time," he directed. "If you bite me, you'll get a worse slap than before. Do you understand?" She glanced first at Daniel, who nodded slightly, then she turned her eyes on Dounton and glared at him. "Aye," she answered.

Satisfied, he began to pull strips of the tender meat apart, holding them between thumb and first finger in a way that she had to accept his fingertips into her mouth. She fought to keep her gorge down, gagging audibly. She was ashamed to have Daniel witness her degradation, and the sucking sounds of her own mouth sickened her. Her grey eyes bore into him with more hatred than she'd ever had for anyone.

After Daniel wrings your neck, may you burn in hell, you vile turd, she thought vehemently.

"Good girl," Dounton praised, slowly withdrawing his fat fingers from her mouth a last time. "Now feed Eames the rest."

Chapter Thirteen

With the repulsive taste of Dounton's grimy fingers still on her tongue, she fed Daniel the remaining turkey. Dounton appeared to lose interest in them and rejoined Corwin and the three hounds at the fire. She was suddenly reminded of Riff.

"Daniel, what happened to Riff?"

He peered at her through his swollen eyes. "Those three beasts surrounded him, but for sport, Corwin called them off. Last I saw, he was limping off into the rushes. Corwin fired a shot, and I've not seen him since."

A fresh wave of sadness washed over her. Poor Riff. He had been such a loyal friend. Deep in mourning the loss of the faithful dog, she barely heard Daniel's whispered words.

"Mary," he was whispering. "Put your hand on my left boot."

Puzzled, she glanced quickly back at Corwin and Dounton, who appeared to be lounging for a moment before they moved on. Dounton puffed on his pipe, casting a lascivious look her way that made her want to retch. Casually, she placed her bound hands on Daniel's boot. She pressed down firmly, and felt something hard and linear. Her eyes widened with realization and she mouthed *my knife?*

He nodded slightly, and added in a low voice, "Took it from you while you were in the throes of the fever. They saw my knife and seized it, but they missed yours. We're in no position to act now, but when I tell you, be ready to use it."

She swallowed hard and nodded. Was there a chance after all? At the mention of her illness, she remembered the cruel words he'd said after she woke from her fever. "This morning," she prompted softly. "Why did you speak so hatefully?"

He scowled as if he didn't understand what she meant. At last he said, "While I was tending to you, you called me Noah."

This horrified her, and she crept closer to him. "Oh, Daniel! Forgive me. In my delirium I knew not what I was saying."

His eyes softened briefly. "I know," he said. "And I beg your forgiveness for my harsh words."

She leaned in to kiss him, but the moment was broken when the dogs rose up and began howling excitedly. Corwin and Dounton got to their feet and glanced expectantly upriver. Mary and Daniel turned to see two canoes gliding silently towards them, each manned by a stern-faced Indian. They approached the river bank, speaking amicably to Corwin and Dounton, who pulled the boats up onto the bank. Dounton strode over to the horses who grazed saddleless nearby. Corwin was already throwing their provisions into one of the canoes when Dounton returned and handed the reins to the Indians. Dounton headed toward them, a large knife in his hand. Mary gasped, recognizing it belonged to Daniel. Dounton sneered at them before he cut the ropes that bound Daniel to the tree. "On your feet, the both of you," he snarled. "Into the canoe. We're Hereford bound."

Mary shot Daniel a helpless look as the ropes securing him to the tree fell away. Dounton cut the ropes that bound Daniel's legs then yanked him to his feet. The Indians watched with disinterest while the three hounds bounded obediently into one of the canoes, again bringing gentle Riff to mind, and Mary's heart ached at the memory of the gentle beast.

Daniel stepped into the empty canoe, the little craft swaying on the shallow water. Seated in the boat, he glared at Dounton, who cradled Mary in his arms like a child before placing her in the boat. He nuzzled her neck, and she shuddered, repulsed by his touch. After sitting her down, his hands lingered on her shoulders, and she fought the nausea that threatened her stomach.

Corwin tossed the provisions in the boat with the dogs before seating himself with his musket across his chest. Dounton tied the two canoes together and resumed his post as Corwin's oarsman. Then Corwin handed Daniel's knife to one of the Indians, apparently concluding some transaction. The Indians shoved them off and waited until both canoes were adrift before they flung themselves onto the horses' bare backs and disappeared into the forest.

While Dounton paddled, Corwin sat facing Mary and Daniel. Her back was to Corwin as she fixed her anguished eyes on Daniel. She noticed his breathing was a bit shallow, and suspected Dounton had cracked a rib when he kicked him. She wished his hands weren't tied behind him so at least they could embrace. His red curls stirred in the warm breeze and she studied every feature of his battered face. She wanted to kneel in front of him but was afraid to upset the canoe, possibly drowning them both. Surprisingly, her eyes still contained tears to shed, and she clasped her hands to her bosom as if in prayer.

"Daniel, what do you think they will do to us?" she whispered anxiously.

He'd been glaring at Corwin, but when his gaze shifted to hers, the coldness subsided. "At best, a trial before they hang us."

Her spirits plummeted. Couldn't he at least give her some encouragement? She stared at her doeskin-covered lap. The rabbit blood stains had darkened to a dark umber. Her moccasins had worn through in spots and strands of hair were working their way loose from her braids. She thumbed tears away from her sunburned cheeks and gave in to a sense of utter hopelessness.

"Even going against the current," Dounton called over his shoulder, "We're making good time. At this pace, we could reach Hereford by sunup."

At this news, Mary slipped carefully from her seat to a kneeling position. The canoe tottered, and she stopped to balance herself. She crept towards Daniel, whose green eyes locked on hers. Kneeling before him she wrapped her arms around his waist and sobbed into his chest.

"Sit down, Miss Mary," Corwin scolded. "You'll upset the canoe and drown you both."

"I'd rather drown embracing you," she said to Daniel, "than see Hereford again."

She remained cradled between Daniel's legs the rest of the night, ignoring Corwin and Dounton's taunts. At one point a wolf howled and the bloodhounds responded with attentive bellows of their own. Mary tuned out everything except Daniel, searing into her memory every facet of his being. As dusk approached, she felt herself grow weary. With her head resting on Daniel's thigh, she gazed up at the moon. It had been full the night she freed Daniel from the jail, and now it was beginning to wane. It seemed to her like an hourglass, and by the time the last sliver of moon disappeared, their lives would be over. She fought back a sob and wondered if either of them would live to see another full moon.

The canoe lurched forward, jostling Mary awake. She'd fallen asleep, still reclining on Daniel's legs. It had been an awkward position to sleep in, and her neck and shoulders were painfully stiff. The sun was well above the horizon, and her heart sank as she recognized the little docks in Hereford. Young men fishing along the riverbank paused when they saw the two canoes gliding upstream. They left their poles and ran into the town, calling excitedly. Soon a crowd of citizens gathered along the riverbank, gawking at the captured fugitives. Old women scowled and shook their heads derisively. Three magistrates regarded the returned fugitives with disdain. Only Constable Absalom Hart's expression bore a hint of empathy. He stood with his young deputy, both armed with muskets. Next to him stood Noah Parker, his wide, sullen face a quiet thundercloud of disapproval. His small nose seemed a bit off-center, and Mary smirked, imagining it was the result of Daniel's strike. Beside Noah stood Reverend Richard Case, staring at her with a look of sheer disbelief.

Mary swallowed, but the lump of fear in her throat wouldn't budge. She pressed firmly against Daniel until the canoe was pulled ashore and Corwin pulled her up by the arm.

"Nephew!" he called cheerfully to Noah as he dragged Mary towards the waiting crowd, "I've found your betrothed!"

She glanced back to see Dounton extract Daniel from the canoe. She wanted to call out to him, but he was hustled away by the constable and deputy. Corwin shook her arm forcefully and said, "Behold your intended, Miss Mary, and your father!"

She couldn't bring herself to look at either her father or Noah, and fixed her eyes on her own moccasined feet. Dounton approached with the knife and cut the ropes from her wrists. As they fell away, she rubbed the reddened, chafed skin.

Noah approached her in three angry strides. He seized her jaw and forced her to look up into his small cold eyes. She loathed his touch as much as she did Dounton's and resentment heated her face.

"Thank you, Uncle," Noah replied, his eyes taking in her doeskin attire with blatant disgust. He released her jaw as Richard stepped closer, shaking his head in dismay.

"Daughter, what has that felon done to you? He's turned you into a veritable heathen."

To her own surprise, she straightened her shoulders and raised her chin defiantly. In a quavering voice, she said, "I want to see Lizzie."

The crowd murmured excitedly and seemed to press closer together lest they miss a single thing. She held Noah's gaze defiantly as Richard stated, "Elizabeth was stricken when she learned of your abandonment. She's recovering at Widow Aker's."

Mary recalled Widow Aker, a toothless old midwife whose small hut was kept in a state of total squalor. Hereford's chimney viewer had fined her many times for not getting her chimney swept and soot covered everything in her home. Despite the state of her abode, Widow Aker was revered as a wise and trusted healer.

The thought that Lizzie suffered a fit due to her own actions unsettled her stomach. "I want to see her," she repeated, the tremor in her voice more pronounced.

"I'm afraid not, Daughter," Richard said. "Seeing you could easily provoke another episode. You'll be detained in the rectory."

Despite herself, she gasped in shock. "Father!" She wanted to ask where Daniel had been taken, but Noah motioned for some of the town matrons to approach. They regarded Mary with a sort of curious revulsion. "Goody Ellis and Goody Hawkins will escort you to the rectory; get you out of those heathen clothes and into some proper attire."

The crowd began to migrate into town, all eyes fixed on Mary as the two matrons escorted her down the familiar streets of Hereford. At first she lowered her head, and then reminded herself, *I am no longer the girl they knew. I've been truly reborn, and I am not one of them.* She raised her chin and inhaled deeply, keeping her eyes trained straight ahead as she walked the gauntlet of hateful jeers and cruel laughter.

Chapter Fourteen

As Mary and her escorts entered the courtyard, the stocks, pillory and whipping post came into view. Her stomach roiled at the thought of Daniel facing the pillory again, or worse, the whipping post. She wondered briefly if she would face one of those brutal punishments herself. She squeezed her eyes shut and willed the thought out of her head.

The rectory door opened with its familiar creak, and the subtle odors of her father's pipe smoke and leather-bound books invaded her nostrils. The small rectory looked the same. Her father's oaken bible box sat prominently on the table and her sewing basket perched on the hearth like a big, contented cat. She noticed the shears that had been missing were lying on top. She continued to survey her old surroundings while Goody Ellis and Goody Hawkins coaxed the glowing embers in the hearth into a pleasant fire and hung a large kettle of water over it.

"We'll have you cleaned up and looking presentable in no time," Goody Ellis murmured as she fetched a basin and mirror. She was the older of the two matrons and she ordered Goody Hawkins, "Look in that trunk yonder for some proper vestments for Mary." She turned to Mary and gently eased her onto the hearth next to her sewing basket. "Remember how you love to sew? It'll be awhile before the water's boiling, so pick up this frayed hem—see? No doubt you could have that mended by the time the water heats."

"Esther," Goody Hawkins said, peering over the open trunk lid. "I can only find a shift and a pair of stays, but no coif."

Goody Ellis huffed. "Anne, check the parlor. I'll look with you. She'll need some salve for those wrists, too. Mary, you just warm yourself by the fire and get reacquainted with your sewing…"

Although my surroundings were familiar, I felt decidedly lost and alienated. I resented the matrons' patronizing demeanors, for it was as though I'd stepped into a new and exhilarating life, only to be viciously pulled back into the old life of mandatory prayers and mundane tasks.

As my indignation grew, I spied the basin and hand mirror on the table. I rose and my moccasined feet made no sound on the wood floor as I approached it. I picked up the little mirror, surprised at my appearance. I had the same grey eyes and rabbit-like overbite. What did the Indian women call me? Wàbòz Ikwe. I did indeed look like a heathen woman, my sunburnt face darkened with filth. Loose hairs had escaped the once-neat braids, and Alawa's bereaved face came to mind. I too had a loss to grieve, and I looked from my reflection to the pair of shears in my sewing basket. Yes, I decided. I too had a right to mourn.

Goody Ellis returned to the hall with her arms full of Mary's old clothing. Goody Hawkins trailed behind her like a chick after its mother hen, the pot of ointment in her hand. "What is that horrid smell—*Mary!* What have you done?"

Goody Ellis dropped the armful of clothing, her toothless maw hanging open. Behind her, Goody Hawkins mirrored her horrified expression, the pot of ointment hitting the floor with a dull *thud.* Both women gasped as they looked at Mary in horror.

She stood before them defiantly with her hair shorn from her head, her two braids like a pair of serpents writhing in the hearth's flames.

After the matrons recovered from their initial shock, they resumed their appointed task. They stripped Mary of her leather tunic, beaded belt and moccasins, throwing them carelessly aside. They scrubbed her face and combed her shorn hair, attempting to engage her in conversation, but she remained silent, staring straight ahead.

The clean linen shift was thrown over her head and a set of stays was tightened around her ribcage. She immediately missed the freedom of the leather tunic, and her feet felt like captives themselves when they'd covered her legs in woolen stockings and encased her feet in her old pair of shoes. Lastly, they covered her hair with a clean coif, lacing it tightly beneath her chin.

"There now," Goody Ellis said, eyeing Mary with approval. "Presentable, just as I promised. "Anne, go fetch the minister and tell him he may enter and behold his daughter."

Anne complied, hurrying out the door. She disappeared from the rectory, returning with both Reverend Case and his assistant reverend in tow. They appraised Mary's transformation scornfully, and she returned their gaze with all the emotion of a fence post.

"Much better," her father said. "Well done, Goodwives. You are excused."

The two matrons nodded, exiting the rectory without another glance back at Mary. Noah eyed her smugly as Richard said, "The Sabbath approaches, and I need time to consider your penance. Before you break your fast, I'll have Noah escort you to the meetinghouse. It needs a good sweeping and dusting, and after you've finished, we'll have prayers."

She remained mute as Noah grabbed her arm and led her into the meetinghouse. It too bore familiar sights and smells. The All-Seeing Eye of God glared judgmentally from the pulpit. The sight of that unblinking eye used to evoke fearful disobedience from her as she'd listen to her father's sermons. Now she resisted the urge to stick her tongue out at it like a defiant child.

Once the door was closed behind them, Noah handed her a broom and dust pan. "Get to work, love," he said smugly. "The sooner you finish, the sooner you can eat."

Her face flamed with indignation as she accepted the implements. He seated himself on one of the backless pews, folding his arms over his chest. She began to sweep in earnest, only because she was filled with so much rage she couldn't stand still.

"I'm the only one who suspects your true involvement in this sordid affair," he said. "And only I can save you from the gallows. You did, after all, poison poor Dirby."

She wished she could shut her ears like she could shut her eyes. She refused to react to his goading statements, and focused on the rasp of the broom's bristles against the knotty pine floor. His voice contained a whining quality that always annoyed her, but now it grated unbearably on her nerves. When she didn't respond, he prodded, "Do you want to hang for your crimes, or will you take advantage of this offer of salvation?"

A pile of dirt was beginning to form and she shaped it neatly in the center of the aisle. Angry words simmered just behind her lips, but she swallowed them down. When she continued to ignore him, Noah rose from his seat and grabbed her arm. "Answer me, Mary!"

She glared first at his pink, knobby-knuckled hand, then looked up into his face. "Let go of me," she hissed finally. "I can't bear the sight of you, much less your touch."

Noah released her arm, but continued to hold her gaze. "So you are that infatuated with the scoundrel you're willing to give your life?"

She shook her head in exasperation and resumed her sweeping, but Noah apparently wasn't finished. "Your father will have you grovel before the congregation for forgiveness this Sabbath, but I can lessen that impending humiliation at least."

Shut up, shut up, shut up! Her mind screamed at him. It would be easier to think of what to do if he would just stop his insipid ramblings.

She heard him extract some papers from his doublet and unfold them. "I've taken the liberty of penning a most repentant confession for you. All you need do is sign it. The magistrates will of course demand a hearing, but with my eloquent words, you could survive this."

"I'll sign nothing," she muttered.

"And after you've signed the confession, we will announce our bann to be married in two weeks' time."

He's mad, she thought. "I'd rather hang and spend two eternities in hell before I marry you."

"Mary," he chided. "Who else now will have you, now that Eames has ruined you? Accept my proposal, and your lover's life may also be spared."

The rasp of the bristles stopped abruptly. *He can't mean that,* she assured herself. She stooped to sweep the pile of dirt onto the dust pan. When she stood upright and turned for the door, Noah was so close behind her she bumped into him, spilling the gathered filth back onto the floor. He smiled wickedly, knowing he had her interest.

"Marry me," he continued, "and I'll see to it Eames is delivered from the gallows and sent back from whence he came."

So that was it, she thought. Daniel's life would remain intact if she gave in to Noah's demands. All her rage and indignation subsided for a moment as she found herself considering his proposition. She would rather suffer a life with Noah and know Daniel was alive somewhere than see him hang.

"Pray, why do you want so badly to marry me? You don't love me."

He brushed her question aside with a careless sweep of his hand.

"Do you swear upon all that's holy that no harm will come to Daniel if I marry you?"

He grinned with satisfaction. "I'm an ordained minister," he reminded her. "My word is gold."

"And Lizzie? I want access to my sister."

"Of course. I'll take you to her after morning prayers."

Her life would be one of misery and heartache, but Daniel would be alive. She would suffer a loveless marriage, but it would be worth the sacrifice, and she would be near Lizzie. Her shoulders sagged in defeat as she herself say, "Aye, Noah. If it will save Daniel's life, I'll marry you."

Chapter Fifteen

Oh Kezia, the depths into which my heart plummeted were immeasurable! Although I was quite famished, I couldn't bring myself to eat the eggs and ham one of the matrons later prepared for me.

Widow Aker's tiny clapboard hut was a good mile out of Hereford, and although the meandering path to her abode had been traversed many times without incident, Noah insisted on toting his musket on his shoulder, perhaps in some pretense of protecting me from any attackers, but part of me suspected it would be used on me lest I try to flee. We walked in unnerving silence, and my only solace was that I would soon see Lizzie.

We could smell Widow Aker's chimney smoke before her dwelling came into view, and I could tell by the scent she was rendering fat for candles and soap. A small stream gurgled pleasantly behind her cottage, offering soothing resonance Widow Aker's patrons found comforting. Upon Noah's knock, the door opened and the toothless old midwife greeted us cheerfully enough. She had once been accused of being a witch herself but somehow her life was spared, and I couldn't remember the details. This reminded me that Daniel said he and his mother had been accused of witchcraft, and my heart ached at the thought of him.

"Come in, come in!" Widow Aker invited, opening the door wide. Both Noah and Mary had to duck their heads to pass through the low entrance, and once inside the stuffy little house, Mary's eyes stung from smoke. Beef fat simmered in a large cauldron, steam billowing into the room. Dried herbs hung in bunches from the rafters and small vials of potions and physicks cluttered the table. Mary recognized the apothecary's bottle of motherwort tincture, and without greeting the old woman, she demanded, "Where is Lizzie?"

Widow Aker regarded her with cataract-clouded eyes. "For sure you want to see your sister," she nodded. "She sleeps the sleep of the blessed. Just gave her a measure of that motherwort potion."

Blinking against the smoke's sting, Mary saw a small figure lying on a pallet in the far corner. The little face framed in a white coif was pale and thin, but definitely Lizzie's. She crossed the room and knelt beside her little sister, horrified at the sight.

"Wake up, Little One," she cooed, shaking her sister gently.

Lizzie's blue eyes fluttered open, glassy and unfocused. Recognition flickered in them, and the little girl's voice slurred sleepily, "Sister? Where have you been?"

"I was away, my darling girl," Mary said, pulling the listless child into her arms. "I've returned and shan't leave you ever again."

Lizzie closed her eyes and smiled. "I missed you."

"I missed you too, Lizzie."

Mary embraced the child, breathing in her sweet scent. She glanced over her shoulder at Widow Aker and Noah, who looked on impassively. Lizzie had never been this listless after taking her morning tincture, and she suddenly thought to ask, "Are you giving her the proper dosage, Widow Aker?"

"Aye," the old woman replied from her hearth, where she slowly stirred the huge kettle of fat. "That and then some. Ensures no fits, and she sleeps much of the day, so I'm free to come and go on my errands."

Something heavy and solid plummeted into Mary's stomach. "You leave her in this stupor *alone?*"

"Now, Mary," Noah chided, seating himself at the cluttered table. "That's no way to speak to an elder. Apologize to Widow Aker at once."

"I won't!" Mary declared, clasping Lizzie even tighter as her outrage grew. "Widow Aker, how *dare* you keep her in such a listless state for your own convenience? And to leave her unattended—I won't have it! I'm sure if Father knew, he would agree with me."

Widow Aker scowled from the hearth. "Such ingratitude, and I asking for no compensation taking this poor child in!"

Mary set Lizzie down gently and got to her feet. "Where is your hartshorn?" She strode to the cluttered table and searched among the plethora of bottles and vials before she found it. She removed the cap and returned to Lizzie's side. Kneeling, she lifted the sleepy girl's head up and waved the ammonia under her nose. Lizzie's eyes fluttered open again.

"She needs something to eat," Mary stated, recapping the hartshorn . "What have you to eat in this hovel?"

Widow Aker glared at her, clearly offended now. "There's remnants of last night's pottage here." She gestured to a smaller kettle hanging on a pot hook over its own small fire. "Feed her then, and begone. I should have insisted on payment had I known I'd be spoken to in this way."

Ignoring the indignant old woman's words, Mary said, "Noah, bring me that kettle. I'll feed her myself."

Noah complied, and she fed Lizzie spoonfuls of the lumpy, bland gruel, gently scraping traces of the pottage from the little face with the wooden spoon. With nourishment in her stomach, Lizzie's eyes focused more clearly and her face crumpled into tears. "Oh, Mary, don't leave me again!"

"I won't, Little One," she promised as Lizzie threw her spindly arms around Mary's neck. She looked meaningfully at Noah. "Let's return her to the rectory."

He shook his head. "Your father knows nothing of this visit, and he's left strict orders that Lizzie is to remain here."

"But she's being mistreated!"

At this, Widow Aker snorted indignantly. "Begone the both of you! And tell Reverend Case I'm charging two pence a day for the girl's lodging."

Noah strode across the little room. "My apologies, Widow Aker. We'll not bother you anymore. Mary, come along now."

Lizzie's eyes widened. "Don't leave me again!" she repeated, clutching Mary's shoulders.

"Mary, we have an agreement," Noah said patiently, prying the sisters apart from their embrace.

Mary bathed Lizzie's little face in quick, frantic kisses. "Forgive me, Lizzie! I'll return when I can."

"Not to this house will you return," Widow Aker muttered.

Noah grabbed Mary's arm, pulling her forcefully out the door. She glanced back at her tearful little sister, arms still outstretched. "I love you, Little One!"

Before she could hear Lizzie's reply, Widow Aker had risen from the hearth and slammed the little door shut.

Noah headed back to Hereford, clearly embarrassed by Mary's outburst. "For shame, to speak thus to an elder," he chided. "And to get your own sister so upset, she's likely to have one of her fits."

Mary could barely breathe over the tightness in her chest. The trees were taking on their most glorious autumn hues now, but she barely noticed. Frustrated and heartsick, she kept her eyes on the ground, lost in her own world of misery. "You promised I would have access to Lizzie."

"Mayhap we'll visit when Widow Aker is out on her errands. She never latches her door, you know," he suggested easily.

Who leaves a child in such a state unattended? She thought, clenching her fists at her sides. *That old hag can barely see to measure the tincture, and Lizzie could easily meet the same fate as Dirby.*

Noah put out an arm and she walked into it, jarring her from her thoughts. "Sh, Mary," he said, stopping to place his musket on his shoulder. "Be still a moment."

Her eyes followed the musket barrel, and something dark moved between the trees. She stood next to him with her fingers in her ears, waiting for the loud report. Then an emaciated black dog emerged from the trees, favoring a front leg. Almost too late, she recognized the animal and shoved Noah's arm, raising the barrel upwards.

"NO!"

The musket fired into the sky, the blast startling birds from nearby trees. Noah looked at her with exasperation. "What the devil--?"

"Riff, oh come here, good darling boy!" she called softly, squatting on her knees with her arms outstretched. The dog looked warily from her to Noah and back again before he limped closer, placing his front paws on her shoulders and licking her face. She rubbed his matted fur, startled at how his ribs stuck out. "Oh, darling boy! I'm so happy to see you!"

Noah snorted. "Eames' dog," he said. At his words, Riff looked up at him and bared his teeth, emitting a threatening growl.

"Daniel languishes in the jailhouse as before, does he not?" she asked, burying her face in the dog's neck.

"Of course," he said, stepping away from the dog.

"I want to reunite him with Riff."

Noah shook his head, but she continued to plead her case. "You've already won, Noah. In two weeks' time we'll be wed. Do this, and I'll never speak of Daniel again."

He seemed to consider this, keeping his distance from the dog. "All right. But mind that mangy thing. He looks like he could rip out my throat."

Mary smiled, thrilled at the prospect of seeing Daniel, if even for the last time. She appreciated Noah's fear of the dog and envisioned Riff tearing him from limb to limb. She patted the dog and he followed alongside her, glancing back at Noah with his ears back. He growled deep in chest, and Noah took two steps back.

Good dog, Mary thought with some satisfaction.

Chapter Sixteen

Dear Daughter, to know Riff was alive was a soothing balm to my aching heart. Despite Father's vehement protests, I insisted on tending to the ailing dog. I fed him some beef scraps, filled a basin of water so he could quench his thirst, and then I tended to his injured leg. The sweet dog allowed me to wash the leg, treat it with salve and wrap it in a linen cloth. Oh, how soulful and sad were those big brown eyes! He thanked me with wet dog kisses as I took an old hair brush and groomed his matted coat. Lastly, I retrieved the beaded belt from the pile of discarded doeskin garments and tied it around his shaggy neck. A more devoted and faithful dog I would never know.

Riff's presence strengthened her resolve, and after she finished tending to the dog, she turned to face Noah with her jaw set and her shoulders back in defiance. "Take me to Daniel now."

"All in good time," Noah replied, keeping his distance from Riff. Producing the confession he'd written, he placed it on the board and said, "Sign this first."

"Only if you swear that before the ink dries, you'll take me to Daniel."

Giving Riff a wide berth, Noah crossed the room to the hearth and retrieved a quill and ink pot. He set the ink pot on the board so loudly Mary jumped. "As you wish. Now sign it."

With Riff at her side, she approached the board and took a seat on the bench. She perused the confession with increasingly watery eyes until her vision blurred, obscuring the words:

I, Mary Case, on this date do declare before Almighty God and Their Majesty's appointed magistrates, that I did willingly bring about the death of Thos. Dirby in an attempt to free the felon Daniel Eames. I then willingly fled with said felon and was in his company for many days. I most humbly beg forgiveness for my grievous and sinful actions.

She dipped the quill with a shaking hand, and the scrape of it on the parchment grated on her ears as she wrote her signature. Not bothering to blow on the ink nor replace the quill in the ink pot, she got to her feet and glared at Noah. "There. Now, take me to Daniel."

Noah scoffed derisively. "Not yet. I've business to attend to elsewhere and it will have to wait until I return. I've arranged to have Constable Hart keep an eye on you until we return. After which, mayhap I'll allow you to visit your lover a last time."

Fury began to burn within her. She'd been a fool to think his word meant anything. He never intended to let her visit Daniel. She was so angry she couldn't speak, and she twisted her apron in her clenched fists until the fabric tore. His betrayal left her shaking, and she was about to reach out and slap him when someone rapped on the rectory door. Noah opened it and Constable Hart stood with a musket in his arms. He nodded a greeting to Noah and gave Mary that same sympathetic look he did when she and Daniel arrived.

Retrieving the signed confession from the board, Noah blew on the ink before folding the paper and tucking it into his doublet. "Watch her carefully," he said to Hart. "Reverend Case is in the meetinghouse, deep in preparation for the coming service. I'm to see my uncle and Mr. Dounton off and should be back within three hours."

At this news, Mary cocked her head curiously, mildly pleased that the two repugnant men would be leaving Hereford. Noah seemed to notice the look of relief on her face and added, "They'll be back within a fortnight. They've gone to fetch witnesses for Eames' prosecution."

I thought I had reached the depths of desperation, but those words sent me into such despair, I could only stand there with Riff pressing his big head against my leg, whimpering softly. Noah left with Constable Hart stationed just outside the rectory door. I ached to see Daniel. I opened the small casement window next to *the door, and stood on my tiptoes to peer out at Absalom Hart. I didn't know him very well, but something told me he might prove to be an ally. The September breeze blew pleasantly into the rectory as I took a deep breath to address my sentry.*

"Constable," Mary called softly as the young man seated himself on a barrel. "Will you speak with me?"

He turned sad, guarded eyes on her, looking slightly surprised. "Nay, Miss Mary. I'm not to speak with you."

"I didn't mean to poison Jailer Dirby. Surely you believe me."

He fidgeted on the barrel, his musket leaning against his thigh. His sad face seemed to grow even more somber. She held her breath in anticipation of his answer. When none seemed forthcoming, she tried again.

Mary bit her lip, thinking hard. Then she heard herself say, "Absalom, you strike me as a sensitive fellow, and I know you have experienced heartache in your life. Am I right?"

He looked away, then met her eyes again. "Pray, close that casement, Miss Mary."

Her fingertips pressed firmly into the windowsill. She felt that her words had snagged on something of value. Wetting her lips, she continued. "Absalom, I beseech you, Daniel Eames is nothing like Noah and the others portray him to be. If you have ever been in love, would you see it fit to escort me to the jailhouse, so I might see him once more? Noah says he will but I don't believe him--"

To her surprise, Constable Hart got up from the barrel, musket in hand. He strode up to the window until their faces were only inches apart. Hope swelled within her until he said, "Mind your fingers." With that, he pushed shut the casement.

The flicker of hope was quickly doused, and she sank again into despair. Absalom Hart might be a sensitive man, but he was also one of honor, and he wouldn't go against his code of ethics. Mary brought her clasped hands to her mouth and gnawed thoughtfully on a knuckle. Riff looked up at her expectantly.

"What shall I do, Riff? We must get to Daniel, and quickly before Noah returns."

Riff cocked his head and answered her with a sad whine.

She paced in frustration, wringing her hands. Riff paced with her, his flat pink tongue lolling to one side. The large box that housed her father's Geneva Bible sat next to the hearth, and on her second pass across the room, she stubbed her toe on it.

"God's eyes!" she cursed, stooping to pick it up. It felt empty, but as she lifted it to set on the board, she felt something shift. Curious, she gently shook the box from side to side.

"Mayhap Father has some notation inside," she said to Riff. But when she lifted the lid, the box was empty. She shook it again, and something definitely shifted.

Intrigued, Mary set the box on the board and seated herself on the bench. "Riff," she whispered excitedly, "there's a false bottom!" Carefully, she pried the bottom up with her fingertips and gasped. A folded sheet of parchment lay within. Riff nudged her elbow, and she absently patted his head with one hand while the other reached for the curious square of paper. She unfolded it and her eyes widened as they scanned the note, written in her father's small, precise hand:

> *Last Will and Testament of Rev. Richard Case*
>
> *On this seventh day of March in the Year of Our Lord 1693, I bequeath unto my daughter Mary's lawful husband, Noah Parker, the sum of £ 500 upon the establishment of their marriage. This nullifies any last Will and Testament I have penned prior to this date.*
>
> *Richard Case*
> *Noah Parker, witness*
> *Sir Humphrey Bead, attorney at law*

Mary stared without comprehension at the document. Noah and her father hadn't met until the Case family arrived in Hereford last May. According to the strange note, the two men knew each other at least two months before that. Mary frowned thoughtfully, trying to digest this information. Her ailing mother was dying, and in early March she remembered her father leaving her to care for both her mother and Lizzie. They lived in Windsor then, and he had applied for the minister's position in Hereford two weeks before. Mary was administering Lizzie's motherwort tincture to her mother in an attempt to ease her pain, but had run out. That afternoon, Richard said he'd walk to the apothecary and get more.

Mary's head began to throb, remembering that awful time. Inexplicably, her father did not return home until the next afternoon, looking more haggard and melancholy than before he'd left. He knelt beside his wife's bedside, holding her hand while Mary gave her mother a few drops of tincture. Weeping, he begged for his wife's forgiveness as she breathed her last.

Tears spilled down her cheeks as she squeezed her eyes shut against the memory of a traumatized Lizzie convulsing on the floor. Shaking the disturbing vision from her mind, she scowled at the paper. What did Noah have to do with any of this?

Riff broke her reverie with a soft yip as he eyed the door. She heard approaching footsteps. Quickly, she folded the document and hurried to return it to its hiding place.

"I trust all is well, Absalom?" her father was saying, just outside the door.

"Aye, sir," Constable Hart replied. "She's within."

She jumped as Richard unlatched the door. She had no time to replace the paper, and hastily thrust it into her bodice. Riff raised one brow, then the other, eyeing her quizzically as Richard opened the door.

"Daughter," he said, the leather bound Bible in his hands, "I've spoken to the magistrates. Noah will read your confession this Sabbath, and your first penance, I'm afraid, will be three hours in the stocks the following Lecture Day."

He crossed to the board, opening the box and placing the Bible within. Mary watched him, a confusing myriad of emotions vying for control within her. Instead of bowing her head in submission, she took a deep breath and withdrew her father's will from her bodice. His eyes widened with surprise and recognition before he snatched it from her hand. Her eyes remained steadily fixed on his and she said in a quavering voice, "You have some explaining to do of your own, Father."

Chapter Seventeen

O how the color drained from Father's countenance when he saw that document in my hand! He snatched it from my grasp and nearly fell onto the bench beside me. Sweet Riff seemed to sense a shift of tension in the room, for her pressed his large head into my lap and nudged my arm until I commenced stroking him.

"Your mother was suffering so," Father began, staring at the document in his trembling hands. And then he turned his sad face towards me and began a most unsettling tale…

Early March, 1693
Windsor, Connecticut

Reverend Richard Case regarded his dear wife from the door of her bedchamber. Elizabeth Purchas Case lay on her deathbed, a perpetual mask of agony on her once-beautiful face. His daughter Mary could only hold her mother's limp warm hand as the family waited for Death to take their beloved from them. Little Lizzie's grief had worked itself into a series of convulsive fits, and now the child lay asleep in her own little trundle bed next to her mother's.

They'd placed Lizzie's motherwort tincture bottle next to the bed, administering the physick in an attempt to lessen Elizabeth's pain. It was nearly empty, and that afternoon, Richard said, "I'm off to the apothecary to replenish the tincture."

Mary merely nodded, not looking up from her mother's pallid face.

Richard threw on his cloak and shut the door behind him, trudging somberly up the street. Despite the bustle of the town around him, all he could hear was the crunch of fresh-fallen snow under his boots.

He'd been a minister in Windsor for fifteen years, and residents who greeted him on the street that cold March day did so with the respectful tone of one offering condolences. He barely acknowledged them, his heart so pained with grief.

'Twould be the merciful thing to give her a large dose of this potion, Richard thought, suddenly ashamed to realize he was considering poisoning his own wife. But it was unbearable to see her in such misery. *Aye,* he felt. *'Twould be the kindest thing to do.*

The apothecary, a small middle-aged man with a port wine stain splashed across half his face, seemed to understand the solemnity of Richard's predicament and poured the sleep-inducing physick into the waiting bottle. Richard paid for his purchase and began his trek homeward on heavy feet.

Between the rectory and the apothecary was Samson's Ordinary, a small but inviting tavern Richard had never patronized, but a measure of rum might give him the courage to go through with his plan, he thought. His legs seemed to have a mind of their own as they transported him through the doorway of the noisy, smoke-filled tavern.

"Surprised to see you here, Reverend Case," Samson himself said, handing tankards of beer to a barmaid. She smiled pleasantly at Reverend Case before taking the stoups from Samson's hands and delivering them to a pair of gentlemen at a far table.

Richard squeezed in between two strange men, and set the tincture on the bar. He turned his sad grey eyes at Samson. "Just one measure of rum to drive off this winter chill," he said.

Samson merely nodded, and Richard stared forlornly into the drink placed before him, still wrestling with his plan.

"You look a might glum, old man," said the stranger to his left. "Pray, what ails you?"

Richard took a large swallow of rum, his eyes on the apothecary bottle. "Nothing that can be made right."

"What's in that little flask there?" asked the one to his right.

"A physick," Richard replied, eyeing the little bottle sadly. "For my ailing wife."

One of the men put a hand on his back. "Let's find us a quiet corner," suggested the first man. "Looks like you could use a listening ear or two."

Richard protested, saying he had to get back, but found himself propelled by the two men towards a small table barely big enough to accommodate one man, let alone three.

"I'm George Corwin," the first introduced himself. "Visiting my nephew here, Noah Parker."

"Reverend Richard Case," Richard muttered, accepting their proffered hands.

"Now that we're friends, pray, do tell us what troubles you," Noah prompted.

Richard resisted, but they plied him with more rum, until he felt like sobbing and told them of his plan to put Elizabeth out of her misery. The two men listened intently, nodding and commenting at appropriate moments. Richard began to feel relieved, having someone willing to listen to his plight. His tongue loosened after more rum. He told them how he and Elizabeth met, and how her family didn't approve of their union, so the young couple eloped. Her family had money, and wanted her to marry someone with social status and not some young, untried minister. He told them of Elizabeth's illness, and how he was considering let her slip into unconsciousness with the help of the motherwort tincture. He was feeling fuzzy-minded and his words slurred when he said, "The fact my wife came from wealth has nothing to do with my decision, I assure you."

Both men's eyebrows rose with interest. "She comes from wealth, does she?" Noah prompted.

Richard nodded, beginning to sway slightly even though he was seated. "But her father's will leaves nothing to Elizabeth nor I. All goes to our daughters once they marry."

"Pray, how many daughters have you and how much moneyage do you speak of?" Corwin asked softly.

"Only one of marriageable age," Richard said, fingering the apothecary bottle before taking another swallow of rum. "She's in her twentieth year, while the younger is but nine."

"So how much does this elder daughter stand to inherit upon matrimony?" Noah pressed with a slight edge of impatience.

Richard gestured vaguely. "Near five hundred pounds, more or less."

Richard was barely aware that Corwin had risen from the small table. "I'm to take on a new parish in Hereford in two weeks, in hopes of making a new start for my daughters and myself. Leave this sad town behind us."

Within a few moments, Corwin returned with a quill, inkpot and a sheet of parchment. Words scrawled hastily in still-damp ink swam before Richard's bleary eyes as Corwin placed it on the small table in front of him.

"Pray, sign your name to this parchment," Corwin said, placing the quill in Richard's hand.

"What is this paper?" Richard slurred.

"My uncle's memory has lapses, and he won't remember your name after we part ways," Noah Parker explained. "He merely wishes to record it for his own recollections."

Richard scowled, wondering vaguely what all the other writing pertained to, but he complied, and Corwin withdrew the paper before Richard could even blow on the ink.

"I must get back to my wife," Richard said, trying to rise from his seat. Dizziness seized him and he collapsed back onto the bench.

"No hurry, is there?" Corwin said. "I have a quiet room upstairs. "Pray, go lie down til the rum wears off."

It wasn't a great distance from the tavern to the rectory, but Richard did see the sense of resting just for a bit before heading home. The two men guided him up the narrow winding steps to the little room Corwin had rented, and he flopped onto the narrow bed gratefully, drifting into unconsciousness almost immediately.

He awoke the next morning to a bucket of cold water splashed violently onto his face. He gasped, raising his aching head off the damp pillow. Two men stood beside the bed, one holding a sheet of parchment.

"Get up, Reverend," the younger said.

Confused, Richard rose slowly to a sitting position, trying to remember what had transpired the day before. The men were unfamiliar to him, yet even in his sorry condition, he sensed their presence bore maleficent will towards him. Cradling his throbbing head in his hand, he listened as they spoke in harsh, urgent voices.

"We have here a confession signed by you that you did willingly poison your wife, and we will present it to the magistrates unless you do as we say."

These words seemed to jolt some awareness into his rum-soaked brain. Regarding them with speechless disbelief, he remained dumbfounded as the younger one continued his small cold eyes boring into Richard from his square, pasty face.

"I'm going to travel to Hereford myself, and you will take me on as your assistant minister. After an appropriate time, I will announce my intentions to marry your eldest daughter."

Richard remained confused. "Why--"

"For her inheritance, old fool!" Corwin supplied, slapping the back of Richard's head so hard Richard winced in pain.

"I'll keep this document on my person for safekeeping, at least until your eldest daughter and I are wed," Noah Parker said, folding the paper carefully and tucking it into his doublet. "Have we made ourselves clear?"

Slowly, like clouds migrating across the blue sky, Richard began to realize he was being blackmailed. He ran his quaking hands repeatedly over his face, his mouth and throat so dry his tongue felt like a shard of tree bark.

"Stay up here til you can leave under your own power," Corwin advised, handing Richard his hat and the bottle of motherwort tincture. "Then go back to the rectory and do the deed, or not. Matters not to us."

What have I done? Richard's mind demanded. He held the physicks bottle in his hand, turning it over as if he could find an answer to his question written on it somewhere. As the magnitude of what just happened became clear, Richard sank into even deeper despair than before.

Chapter Eighteen

Mary stared at her father, speechless with incredulity. The irony that she had unintentionally brought about Dirby's death in the same way her father had planned to take her mother's wasn't lost on her. She was furious and confused and at a complete loss as to what to do. She knew nothing of her mother's family and had no idea she had an inheritance coming. She opened her mouth, but could form no words.

"Forgive me, Daughter," he blubbered, his hands shaking as he dropped his hat on the board and whisked tears from his cheeks. "I was in a most sorry state, so they arranged for me to speak to a barrister friend of theirs, and I wrote this damnable will."

Richard's instant transformation from stern father to chagrined old man unsettled her. "What am I to do?" she asked helplessly. "Noah said if I agreed to marry him, he'd let Daniel go free."

Richard shook his head. "I wouldn't trust his word on that."

Panic seized her mind. She wanted to scream at her father, but that wouldn't solve anything. She clenched her fists on the table and said, 'Father, Noah will be back in less than two hours. You must take me to Daniel."

He looked appalled. "I can't have you visit that scoundrel--"

"But to save yourself you're willing to marry me off to a worse one!"

Her father's shoulders sagged in defeat and he nodded. "I'll escort you myself to the jailhouse."

Mary exhaled, unaware she'd been holding her breath. She got to her feet, snatched a shawl from its hook and threw it over her shoulders as Richard returned his hat to his head. He rose more slowly and opened the rectory door for her.

It seemed to take an unusually long time before she and Richard crossed the courtyard to the jailhouse. Riff made a mad dash for the little building, wagging his tail excitedly as he waited for them to catch up. Images of the last time she was there flashed through her mind—Dirby's wizened, trusting face lighting up at the sight of the rum jug. She shook the image from her mind and held her breath as the deputy opened the door. Riff made a beeline for the cell, where his master sat. Mary ignored the narrow bed on which Dirby had succumbed to the tincture, her eyes focused only on Daniel who sat in the same position he had before, with his bound wrists clamped to a hook above his head. His eyes were not as swollen as when she'd seen him last but his entire face was still discolored with bruises.

James the deputy looked surprised, then confused, when Richard said, "Please give my daughter some time alone with the detained."

James had his orders. He seemed to want to protest, but finally acquiesced. "I'll be just outside," he said finally, looking from both Richard to Mary and back again. He took his musket and left the room, shutting the door behind him.

Riff whined excitedly, his eyes going from Daniel to Mary, evidently waiting for her to unlock the cell door and let him join his master. Hastily she plucked the key ring from its peg and with shaking hands, unlocked the door. She and Riff both ran into the little cell, she falling on her knees beside him, Riff slathering his master's face with wet dog kisses.

"Daniel," was all she managed to say, kissing his beaten face carefully and inhaling his scent. She wanted to drink him in with all her senses. Her fingers entwined themselves in his matted curls and she buried her face in his neck.

"Riff, down," Daniel managed, and Riff stopped licking his face but remained pressed against his master's side, looking up at him with utter love and devotion. "Mary, what are you doing here?" His eyes slid warily to Richard, who stood outside the cell, fidgeting with his hat in his hands.

"Father, join the deputy outside, pray. I wish to be alone with Daniel."

"Daughter, I can't allow that," he said, and for a moment he had regained his authoritative air. Frustrated, Mary turned to Daniel again. "We haven't much time, but Father has confessed the most horrible thing to me!"

In hurried breaths, she explained the situation and her pending nuptials with Noah. During her narrative, Daniel's eyes slid from her to Richard, who stood shame-faced just outside the cell door. "I only said I would marry him because he promised he would let you go free," she sobbed. "But now I know what a miscreant he is, I know his word is meaningless. Oh, Daniel, I don't know what to do! Please forgive me!" When she finished her tale, she succumbed to the overwhelming despair that crushed her soul like a vise. She threw her arms around his neck and sobbed.

Daniel listened silently, his battered face expressionless except for the fierce glint in his green eyes she'd come to know. Before he could respond, the door burst open, and the deputy ran in, his face pale with fear.

Riff cocked his ears in alarm and looked to Daniel before rising on all fours. The church bell tolled, and excited voices could be heard in the courtyard.

"What's happening?" Mary cried over the din of the church bell.

"Fire!" was all the deputy managed, grabbing the water bucket from beside the desk. "Widow Aker's house is ablaze!" He disappeared out the door, the bucket swinging from his hand.

Lizzie! Dear God, Lizzie is in there! Her mind screamed. She looked to Richard, his face a mask of panic.

"Daughter, let's go at once!"

She didn't want to leave Daniel so soon, but Lizzie needed her. Indecision tugged at conscience in multiple directions. She looked helplessly from Richard to Daniel. Her father hesitated only a moment before he bolted out of the jailhouse after the deputy.

"Daniel, I don't want to leave you, but Lizzie--"

"Cut me loose, Mary!" Daniel demanded, straining at the ropes.

Mary retrieved her knife from Daniel's left boot, tears obscuring her vision already as her fear grew. Just as before, she severed the ropes and when they fell away, Daniel sprang to his feet. He helped her up and she sheathed her little knife, tucking it into her bodice. Then Daniel grabbed her hand and they both raced to the burning house.

A grey plume of smoke climbed ever higher into the sky just outside of Hereford. A bucket brigade had assembled, transporting water from the stream behind Widow Aker's house one bucket at time to the fire.

No! Mary's mind screamed. *Lizzie can't die! Not so young, and so tragically!*

Mary's throat was raw from screaming, and she choked on the heavy smoke as they drew near. Angry, roaring flames devoured the little house despite the valiant attempt to extinguish them. Mary beat at the flames with her shawl, holding her apron over her nose with one hand. The heat baked her face and scorched her lashes.

From her right, Richard dashed into the burning cottage, disappearing from sight.

Over the roar of the fire and urgent cries for more water, Riff barked frantically, and bolted into the house, his shaggy body enveloped in smoke.

"Damn dog!" Daniel muttered under his breath and before Mary could react, Daniel ran into the smoking maw of the doorway.

"Daniel!" Mary cried. *Dear God, I'm going to lose everyone I love!*

"The roof's about to go!" a man shouted.

Mary looked on in horror as the flames consumed the little house despite the futile attempts of the bucket brigade. She fell to her knees and wept into her apron.

"Look!" a voice exclaimed excitedly, jolting Mary from her despair. She lifted her smoke-stung eyes to see four figures emerging. Daniel appeared first, grasping Riff's collar with one hand. A small figure was slung over one shoulder, and behind him, Richard and Widow Aker stumbled out, all of them covered in soot and coughing. Just as they cleared the threshold, the roof gave way in a thunderous roar, sending more flames and smoke skyward. The group collapsed in a heap a safe distance from the destroyed house.

Mary got to her feet and pushed her way blindly towards the survivors just as Daniel gently laid Lizzie down. Mary knelt next to her sister, the little face as soot-covered as the rest.

"Lizzie!" she screamed, shaking the little girl by the shoulders gently at first, then harder. "Lizzie, wake up!"

"Turn her over and slap her back," someone suggested. Mary complied, Lizzie's limp body flopping like a rag doll. She pounded frantically on her sister's back, but Lizzie gave no response. Richard and Widow Aker continued to cough violently, and Daniel's chest heaved as he put a hand on Mary's arm.

"Stop, Mary," he said in a low voice.

"Wake up, Little One!" Mary continued to scream, returning Lizzie to her back. "Please wake up!"

Mary wiped soot from Lizzie's still face, but the girl's pallor remained grey. *No!* She screamed silently, and then she released a soul-wrenching cry of anguish. She clutched Lizzie's limp body to her as shock enveloped her.

Richard's coughing turned into mournful wails, and Riff whined sadly. A woman stepped forward to relieve her of Lizzie's body, and she tightened her embrace.

"Give the child to me, love," Goody Ellis' voice was saying from somewhere far away. "She's gone."

This is a horrid dream, part of her mind insisted as both Goody Ellis and Daniel pried Lizzie from her arms. *This can't be real. Lizzie can't be dead!*

"Mary," Daniel said, finally managing to release Lizzie from her. As Goody Ellis gently removed her sister's body, it felt like her heart was being violently withdrawn from her chest, leaving an empty void. She stared at the smoking remains of Widow Aker's house, and then at Widow Aker. The old woman was on all fours, still coughing the smoke out of her lungs. A rage flared up within Mary, and she turned on Widow Aker, knocking the woman on her back and straddling her. She wrapped her fingers around the old woman's scrawny neck and squeezed.

"You stupid, careless old woman!" she cried, the words ripping painfully from her raw throat. "You killed Lizzie!"

Widow Aker's eyes bulged as she struggled for air. "Mary, stop!" Daniel said, pulling her off her victim. Other women came to Widow Aker's rescue as Daniel turned her against his chest and let her cry. He held her in a firm embrace just as he'd done beneath the canoe.

She peered at her father over Daniel's shoulder. Richard's face wore the same mask of unfathomable grief it had when her mother died. She withdrew from Daniel's arms and crept towards Richard. He opened his arms to her and she fell into them. Together, they succumbed to mutual sorrow and sobbed.

Mary looked up from Richard's shoulder, the sound of hoof beats growing closer. Noah Parker was thundering towards them on a sorrel gelding. He reined the animal in just yards away from where Mary, Richard and Daniel stood. Riff growled, startling Noah's mount so that for a moment he struggled to regain control.

"What's the meaning of this? Why is this man out of his cell?" he demanded, scowling first at Daniel then at Constable Hart.

"As you can see," Hart replied, regarding Noah with his soulful eyes, "There's been a fire. Young Elizabeth Case was lost--"

Noah raised his brow in apparent shock. "My condolences, Reverend Case and Mary. But the Sabbath begins at dusk and this thief must be returned to the jailhouse. I trust you and your deputies will do your duty."

Mary watched this exchange through a dense fog of grief. Shock was slowly numbing her senses, and she looked helplessly at Daniel. His intense green eyes met hers briefly before they steadily settled on Noah with discernable animosity.

"I want to see Eames back in his cell by the time I return from the livery." With that he steered the gelding around and galloped down the winding path to town.

What do we do now? Mary wondered silently, wishing someone would offer a solution to this whole catastrophe. She drew away from Richard as Constable Hart approached Daniel with an almost apologetic look on his face.

"You did a brave and honorable thing, Eames," he said in a low, sincere voice. "I may have to incarcerate you until the upcoming hearing, but I won't bind you. Do I have your word that you'll return peaceably to town with me?"

As the crowd dispersed, Mary stepped closer to Daniel and took his hand. His green eyes glinted like emeralds against his blackened face. Something meaningful and silent seemed to pass between the two men, and Daniel nodded. "That I will."

Constable Hart excused his deputy, who gave him a curious look before obediently heading back to town.

"Reverend Case, Mary…"

They all turned to see Widow Aker, tears leaving streaks on her sooty cheeks. Her dull old eyes were filled with apparent sorrow as she looked at them. "You must know something."

The sight of the old woman sent rage flaring anew within her, but Widow Aker raised a gnarled and quivering hand to hold back any angry words directed towards her. "Constable, the fire 'twas not my fault."

"*Not your fault?*" Mary shrieked in incredulity. "Obviously you were careless rendering fat in that tinderbox of a dwelling of yours! If only you'd been not so careless, my sister would still be alive!"

Widow Aker flinched at the angry words as Constable Hart stepped up. "Let her speak, Mary," he said.

"You can check the remains of my hearth for proof," the old woman insisted. "I'd finished rendering fat yesterday and the kettle sits now in a far corner of the hearth, empty and dry as a barren womb. Indeed, my hearth fire did go out last night, and I meant to borrow fire from Goody Ellis this very morning, but--" her words trailed off as she gestured helplessly at the still-smoking ruin that had once been her home.

Mary and the men exchanged confused looks, and Constable Hart asked, "What are you saying, Widow Aker?"

"I'm saying," rasped the old midwife, "'Twas not my fire that set my poor home ablaze. That fire must surely have been set by someone else."

Chapter Nineteen

Mary stared at Widow Aker, trying to digest this new information. The old midwife returned her gaze with earnest remorse, the cataract-clouded eyes tearing up afresh.

"I'm so deeply sorry for your loss," Widow Aker said softly, laying a gnarled hand on Mary's arm. "Elizabeth was a sweet child."

An unsettling chill descended upon Mary, turning her skin to gooseflesh. She turned to Daniel, who exchanged a look with Constable Hart. "I'll escort you to the jailhouse and assign James to watch you," Hart said to Daniel. "I need to investigate this."

"Allow me to stay, Constable, and you'll have the benefit of Riff's keen senses to help with that investigation," Daniel replied, dropping his branded hand onto Riff's head. The dog looked up at his master with his soulful brown eyes.

Richard was noticeably trembling, and he looked as though his heart had shattered into a thousand shards. "I'd like to stay, to hear the answers you find the moment you find them."

Mary nodded. "I, too, would like to stay."

The constable searched each face, then acquiesced. "Widow Aker, 'twas your home. You can tell us the lay of your dwelling."

"Indeed," the old woman said, removing her hand from Mary's arm. "Follow me."

We walked carefully among the ruins of Widow Aker's dwelling. She pointed out the hearth and the aforementioned kettle. True enough, it sat empty save for the ashes and charred beams that had fallen into it. A singed pallet lay still smoking, and I knew this is where my Lizzie perished. Images of her lying there helplessly made my stomach roil, and I struggled to keep my gorge down. Glass crunched beneath my shoes, and I realized I was walking on smashed vials of herbal concoctions. Riff kept his nose low to the ground, sniffing every inch of the destroyed home. While the men made comments, Widow Aker sobbed into her ash-covered apron. I was still fighting the nausea when Riff took off towards the little stream that ran behind the small house, his black nose still pressed to the ground. None of us paid him much mind until he looked back at us and barked most excitedly....

"I believe he's found something," Daniel said, striding out of the charred ruins with Hart, Richard and Mary close behind him. He knelt beside Riff, who looked pointedly at the stream. "Good boy," Daniel said as the others drew nearer. "Constable, you're going to want to see this."

They gathered to where Daniel pointed. A charred pine knot lay half-submerged in the shallow stream. Constable Hart retrieved the extinguished torch from where it lay and scrutinized it carefully. He handed it to Daniel, and examined the ground for more clues. Mary clasped Widow Aker's hand and held her breath in anticipation.

"Hoof prints," Constable Hart announced, pointing at several clear prints along the footpath. "Appear to be in a hurry, heading into the forest." Turning to the others, he said, "It looks as though he tossed the torch into the stream as he fled the scene."

Richard, who'd remained quiet for so long, finally demanded in a quaking voice, "But whom? Who would want to kill my sweet Elizabeth?"

Mary felt a chill trickle down her spine like a single raindrop. She looked to Daniel, but his face held no answers as he inspected the hoof prints alongside Hart. Then both Daniel and Hart squatted on their heels, examining a particular hoof print.

"See there, this shoe had a large pit in it," Daniel said, indicating a distinct anomaly in one well-preserved print.

Hart nodded, and Mary sensed a harmonious bond solidifying between the two men. They obviously were of the same mind, almost thinking the same thoughts. Hart turned to Mary and asked, "Pardon me, Miss Mary, but will you fetch me a piece of charcoal from Widow Aker's dwelling?"

His request snapped her out of her daze, and she complied, holding a hand over her unsettled stomach as she walked to the smoldering ruins. She plucked a still-warm sliver of charred wood, avoiding the smoldering pallet. Returning to the men, she handed it to Hart.

"Pray, lend me your apron," Hart said, giving her an apologetic look. "Yours too, Widow Aker."

Mary again complied, untying the strings from her waist and handing him the white linen garment. Hart smoothed it out on the footpath next to the clear hoof print and drew a crude sketch of it on the cloth. Then he set the charcoal down and carefully rolled the apron up with the sketch on the inside. Then he retrieved the pine knot and wrapped it carefully in Widow Aker's apron.

"I'll take this to the livery stable, see if any animals boarded there match this print," the constable said as both he and Daniel rose to their full height. "I'm afraid I'll have to return you to the jailhouse first, Eames."

"Understood," Daniel said. "I trust you'll let us know if you match the shoe to that print."

Hart's sullen eyes regarded Daniel earnestly. "Aye," he confirmed. He looked meaningfully at Richard, Mary and Widow Aker. "This can go no further if we're to discover the culprit. Do you all swear to keep this information to yourselves?"

"I swear it," Richard said in a hollow voice.

"I, too," Mary replied.

"Indeed," Widow Aker nodded. "I want nothing more than to find out who destroyed my home."

They walked in uncomfortable silence towards Hereford. Immersed in her own grief, Mary's emotions flitted from deepest sorrow to sheer outrage and back again. Someone had purposely set the fire that killed sweet Lizzie! An invisible fist clenched her heart and her stomach remained upset as they headed towards the jailhouse. By now the citizens had heard of Lizzie's demise, and they cast empathetic glances towards Mary and Richard, but Mary kept her eyes on the ground, biting her lips against the mournful wails that threatened to erupt from her throat.

Constable Hart opened the jailhouse door and the somber party entered. Everything had been as they'd left it, the cell door ajar. Daniel entered the cell, commanding Riff to stay out. The dog whined in protest, but obeyed, planting himself firmly next to Mary. After Hart shut and locked the cell door, Daniel rested his forearms on the bars and Mary took his hands in hers.

"I'll have James watch you," Hart said to Daniel. "I'm off to the livery stable." Looking directly at each face, he reminded them, "Tell no one about the torch and the hoof print."

They all reaffirmed their promise with quiet nods, and the constable left with the concealed pine knot in one hand and the charcoal sketch in the other.

"He's a good man," Richard commented admiringly after Hart left. Turning sullen eyes towards Mary, he said, "We ought to retire to the rectory, Daughter. No doubt the goodwives are…preparing Elizabeth."

The sad visage of Lizzie lying on a table, being washed and shrouded in winding sheets sent her gorge rising, and she clamped her hand over her mouth as she hurried out of the jailhouse. She collapsed on her knees and retched. Someone was hammering something nearby in the courtyard, and the pounding made her head throb. After she'd emptied her stomach of its contents, she looked up to see a pair of men hammering away on something propped on two saw horses. They gave her a pitying look as they stepped aside. She glimpsed what they were making and screamed.

Upon the saw horses rested an achingly small coffin.

Chapter Twenty

My memories of that horrid Sabbath are dull. Normally, Noah would have supped with us that evening, but methinks Riff proved to be a formidable deterrent. Father and I ate in silence, and Father gave the briefest of prayers before we took to our beds. I lay sleepless all night, dreading the coming services. Instead of sweet Lizzie lying beside me, Riff had curled up next to me. I wonder if he smelled her scent on the blankets, for he looked at me with the saddest expression I'd ever seen on a dog's face. He whimpered, and I cried into his shaggy coat until the sun came up.

Mary awoke bleary-eyed, fully dreading the upcoming Sabbath service. After lacing her stays, she opened the trunk and removed an apron that had belonged to her mother. Her fingers stroked the bleached linen reverently, then buried her face in its folds. Her mother's scent still clung faintly to the fabric, conjuring images of her mother's face to form in her mind. Tears slid down her face as she realized she had never properly mourned her mother. Now Lizzie was gone, too. Riff watched her with his large, soulful eyes and whined softly.

Oh Mother, how I could use your guidance now! She thought. *My only solace is that you and Lizzie are reunited.*

Her empty stomach gurgled as she tied her mother's apron around her waist. A kettle of samp was still warm from the night before, but she had no appetite as she spooned it into two bowls. She placed some meat scraps in a bowl for Riff which the dog attacked hungrily. Richard joined her at the board, and bowed his head before offering a morning prayer. Richard's prayer was interrupted by a sharp knock at the door. Puzzled, Richard rose and opened the door to find Constable Hart standing on the rectory stoop, his usual melancholy replaced by startling urgency.

"Forgive the disturbance," Hart said, removing his hat and stepping inside before being welcomed in. "I waited until Parker entered the meetinghouse. I have something of the utmost importance to tell you."

Richard closed the door behind their unexpected guest as Mary rose to greet him. Riff's tail swung in friendly greeting as he nosed Hart's hand, which absently patted the dog's head. As Hart's soulful eyes found hers, a heavy stone dropped into her queasy stomach, and she reseated herself, suddenly feeling dizzy.

"As promised, I inspected all the horses at the stable. I found a match for the hoof prints. Mind you, this was yesterday, before the Sabbath began," Hart clarified, his voice low.

Mary clasped her hands in her lap so tightly her knuckles resembled snow-capped mountain peaks. When neither Mary nor Richard spoke, Hart went on, worrying the brim of his hat. "The prints belonged to a sorrel gelding."

Noah! The realization seemed to hit Richard the same time it occurred to Mary, and they exchanged a stricken glance. Richard swayed, and Hart grasped the minister's arm before gently guiding him to his chair at the head of the board. Riff whimpered softly and rested his snout in Mary's lap. She stroked his neck, fingering the beaded belt.

"He killed my Elizabeth?" Richard muttered in disbelief. "Why? What heartless demon would kill an innocent child?"

Absalom Hart fidgeted uncomfortably. "After my discovery, I relieved my deputy and spoke privately with Eames. He said you might have something to tell me, Reverend."

Richard dropped his head in evident shame, and as her father seemed to crumble before her eyes, she heard herself say in a hollow voice, "The inheritance."

Constable Hart glanced at Mary curiously. Richard appeared to be in no condition to speak, so Mary explained Noah's plot to wed her for her inheritance. "I would have had to share it with Lizzie," she said, her voice cracking at the mention of her sister's name. "That's the only reason I can give for him murdering--"

She dissolved into tears, leaving Constable Hart standing awkwardly amidst a grieving father and daughter. Finally, he cleared his throat and said, "I'll speak to the magistrates in due course. Reverend, you and Mary must not let on that you know of Parker's involvement. Can you compose yourselves and carry on for the day?"

Mary and Richard looked at each other across the board, their faces both pale and tear-streaked. Dark circles shadowed their eyes, but they nodded in unison. But then Richard looked as though he had just remembered something. "Noah will perform Elizabeth's funeral tomorrow!"

Mary hadn't considered that. To have that vile creature speak over Lizzie—the very monster that killed her—worsened her nausea. She looked imploringly from Richard to Hart. "Oh, I can't bear to be near that--"

"That bastard," Richard finished for her, and even though she'd never heard her father curse before, she nodded in agreement, wishing she could have brought the word forth herself.

"I understand," Hart said, "but 'tis imperative you don't let on until I speak with the magistrates." The first peal of the church bell rang out, summoning the parishioners to worship. Hart shot a last urgent glance at both of them. "Now, Reverend, I suggest you and Mary hasten to the meetinghouse. God be with you."

And so Father and I entered the meetinghouse. I felt as though my legs were carrying me of their own accord, like an old horse who knows its way and needs no guidance from its master. Riff acted as my bodyguard,

letting no one approach me as I kept my eyes downcast. I was barely aware of my bench mates as I sat woodenly, willing the sand in the hour glass to fall more quickly. I braced myself to hear Noah Parker's sermon, but the moment he addressed the congregation, my empty stomach revolted and I retched into my apron before sliding off the bench. The last thing I remember is the oaken floor rising up to meet me.

Mary awoke to the taste of bile in her mouth. Goodwives Ellis and Hawkins knelt beside her as she reclined against the wall of the meetinghouse. Goody Ellis' face registered deep concern as she dabbed Mary's face with the corner of her dampened apron.

"Mary, love, how are you feeling? You fainted dead away," Goody Ellis said, regarding Mary with her rheumy eyes.

Before Mary could reply, Riff nudged his snout under her arm and lapped her cheek. Her arm curved around the dog's shoulders as she inhaled his comforting scent. She grew increasingly aware of her audience, and saw her father and Constable Hart watching anxiously from the men's side. Noah descended the pulpit, glowering at Riff, who curled his lips and growled threateningly.

"Get that beast away from her!" Noah thundered, keeping a safe distance. "Constable, chain this animal to the whipping post."

Mary sunk both hands into the shaggy fur and gripped the beaded belt. "No!" she protested as the goodwives rose to allow Constable Hart to approach. He gave her a pleading look, and she could almost hear his silent message, *trust me*. He reached for Riff's collar, muttering encouragements in a low, steady voice until Riff relaxed. Hart gently pried Mary's arms from the dog's shoulders and grasped the belt firmly. With obvious reluctance, the dog was led out of the meetinghouse. Mary missed his reassuring bulk and pulled her cloak tighter around her shoulders as Noah approached.

Not another step closer, you despicable creature! She cried inwardly, fighting the urge to spit at him. Riff's howls of protest rent her heart as Noah offered his hand to her. She cringed, and eyed Constable

Hart returning from securing Riff to the whipping post. She looked imploringly at Hart's somber face, and he offered a hand to her as well.

"Allow me to be of assistance," he said in his steady voice, holding her eyes with a meaningful gaze. She accepted his hand, still ignoring Noah's, who eventually dropped his arm to his side and returned to the pulpit while Constable Hart helped Mary to her feet. She swayed slightly on watery legs, the sanctuary spinning before her eyes. Richard approached, taking her other arm. She glanced from Richard to Hart, trying to steady herself. The tithingman had walked to the pulpit, his hand on the hourglass, prepared to flip it over on Noah's cue.

"My daughter hasn't eaten and is clearly unwell," Richard said to their audience. "Constable Hart and I will take her outside for some fresh air." With that, Mary was escorted down the aisle by both men. She heard the tithingman reset the hourglass with a firm *thump* against the pulpit, and Noah's resonant voice resuming his sermon. As Richard and Hart escorted her out, Riff barked excitedly, straining so hard he started to choke. The big dog gave up, and sat on his haunches, whining imploringly.

The two men gently eased Mary onto a bench that ran along the side of the meetinghouse. The air was taking on the crispness of autumn, and she inhaled deeply, willing her stomach to settle.

"Daughter, could you eat something?" Richard asked softly.

Mary shook her head, her eyes on the bile-stained apron. "Mayhap I've never recovered fully from the fever I suffered while I was with Daniel."

"We ought to return," Hart reminded them, "lest Parker grows suspicious."

Richard nodded in agreement, and both men helped her to her feet. She drew in a final lungful of fresh air and steeled herself to face Noah again. She glanced at the jailhouse, longing to be with Daniel, Riff sent up another plaintive howl, rending Mary's heart anew.

I felt every eye upon me as Father escorted me back to my seat, flanked by Goodwives Ellis and Hawkins. The tithingman had opened the three casement windows in my absence, allowing the breeze to air out the stuffy meetinghouse. From where I sat, I could see the jailhouse, and I longed to be with Daniel.

Noah continued on with his sermon as though nothing was amiss, and I fought the urge to cover my ears in an attempt to shut out his execrable voice. In the courtyard, Riff's lamentable howls persisted, until they progressed into excited barks. The hourglass was nearly empty, and when it was time for midday break, Noah turned an exasperated eye to the tithingman.

"I'll silence that annoying beast, and make it permanent!" Noah declared, pointing in the direction of the barking.

"No!" Mary shrieked as Noah stepped down from the pulpit and produced a large knife from its sheath. She rose to stand, but Goody Ellis placed a firm arm around her shoulders. Too weak to protest further, she collapsed back against the other woman's shoulder, weeping as Noah marched purposefully out the door. Mary covered her ears to keep out Riff's last cries, but instead she heard Noah bellow, "Indians!"

Before the word was fully uttered, blood-chilling war whoops were heard, energizing the entire congregation. Goodwives Ellis and Hawkins rose in unison, propelling Mary to the center of the room with the other women. Mary peered out the window as the men hastened to arm themselves. It took several moments to prepare their muskets against such an unexpected attack. Mary watched transfixed as Noah ran fearfully across the courtyard, his face a mask of sheer terror. Behind him, a warrior took careful aim and sent an arrow into his shoulder. Mary gasped as Noah shrieked, looking imploringly for help.

"Get away from the window!" Hart instructed her, pulling her arm.

But Mary resisted. She stood rooted to the window as the warrior strode towards Noah, his stern face painted a fearsome black and red. His arms and torso were heavily tattooed, and she recognized him.

That's Charles! Mary realized. Muskets were fired, but the Indian was too far away, and the shots only filled the meetinghouse with smoke. Mary's eyes stung and her coughs joined those of others as she watched the Indian deftly sling Noah over his bare shoulders and disappear into the woods, Noah's cries fading away.

What would he want with Noah? Mary thought vaguely. *Surely the Indians don't know of his involvement with Lizzie's murder—*

Two more warriors kicked down the jailhouse door. Amidst smoke and chaos, Mary watched in disbelief as they disappeared inside. Moments later, they emerged with Daniel between them. Another Indian on horseback offered Daniel his arm, and Daniel swung up behind him.

They're rescuing Daniel! This discovery was followed by an overwhelming sense of abandonment. *He's leaving me!*

"Daniel!" Mary cried as the small band of Indians disappeared into the dense forest. "Father, they took Daniel!"

"Cease fire!" Constable Hart ordered. When the men put aside their muskets, they turned to him expectantly.

"We need to rescue Reverend Parker!" a man declared urgently. "And get back Eames!"

Mary's sense of abandonment bloomed like a bloodstain on linen as Hart commanded the congregation to quiet down. His voice, always low and steady, soothed the agitated crowd by a few degrees, but Mary again felt a wave of vertigo hit her and allowed Goody Ellis to walk her back to her seat while Constable Hart stepped up on to the pulpit.

He left me. Those words refrained in her head incessantly as Hart ordered the crowd to be seated.

"It's evident the Indians got what they came for," he began. "Else they would have attacked the congregation."

"We must retrieve Parker and Eames!" the same man insisted, and other men voiced their agreement.

"I'll form a posse post haste," Hart said, his eyes scanning the congregation for members of the local militia. "Arm yourselves, men, and meet me in the courtyard at the utmost soonest."

As the congregation began to clear out, Mary approached Hart, still dizzy and weak. "Absalom, let me go with you."

"Don't be absurd," he told her firmly. "This is no business for a woman, especially one apparently unwell."

"Absalom, please!" Mary begged, but she knew he was right. Richard was soon beside her, offering a steadying arm.

"Daughter, listen to the constable," he urged, his eyes still shadowed with raw grief. "Stay with me."

Absalom's eyes were sincere when he looked at her. "I'll return Eames to you," he said softly. He turned to Riff, who whined imploringly. Absalom knelt before the big dog and removed the rope from his shaggy neck. Riff immediately thanked him with sloppy kisses. Absalom stood upright and stroked Riff's back as he turned to Mary and Richard. "I'll take Eames' dog with me. Mayhap he can help us find his master. Now go with your father to the rectory."

He's a decent, honest soul, Mary thought suddenly, and smiled gratefully at his earnest face.

"Thank you, Absalom," she whispered.

Chapter Twenty-one

Riff's presence was painfully missed. I'd come to draw a considerable amount of comfort from the shaggy beast, and could barely eat nor sleep for the next several days. While I wallowed in this new heartache, Absalom Hart and five of his militia followed the Indians to their camp. Later, the good constable relayed to me what transpired...

Absalom Hart led his posse of five men single-file through the thick brush, dodging low tree branches that threatened to knock him from his mount. A gentle breeze sent yellow and orange leaves fluttering to the sun-dappled forest floor. They reminded Absalom of how much his young wife in New Hampshire had enjoyed this time of year, and how she managed an endless list of chores with a contented smile on her heart-shaped face. Whether Alice was salting fish, dipping candles or sweeping the floor, she never complained.

A lieutenant in the New Hampshire Militia under Major Richard Waldron, Absalom worked diligently at Waldron's grist mill in Dover when he wasn't tending to his own small plot of land along the Cocheco River. A hero from King Phillip's War, Waldron was President of New Hampshire, and controlled Dover as if he were king and the other citizens his serfs. Absalom grimaced with disdain as Waldron's scornful face materialized in his mind's eye.

It was in May of 1689 that Alice came to Absalom, her face

flushed and eyes sparkling when she told him she was with child. The prospect of parenthood delighted them both, and it was a happy time for the Harts.

And then came the awful night of June 27, when the local Penacook tribe raided the settlement, carrying off those they didn't slay with their arrows and hatchets.

Hart squeezed his eyes shut tightly against the horrid memory, breathing in lungfuls of crisp autumn air to clear his head when the young deputy called James spoke, breaking into his reverie.

"If they took to the water, the dog can't track their scent," James remarked as Riff came to the edge of the Great River.

"The dog was with Eames at the Indian camp," Hart replied, his voice tight. "I'm assuming they're returning to the same camp, and Riff here knows where that is."

At the sound of his name, Riff looked back at Hart and yipped in affirmation.

Another member of the posse asked, "So what happens if we're able to return Eames? The townsfolk won't want a hanging, after the fine mettle he displayed at Widow Aker's."

Hart nodded. "I'll speak to the magistrates on Eames' behalf. For now, we'll follow the dog to the Indian camp, and you'll keep your weapons close, but not drawn until I say."

Riff was already ambling purposefully downriver, and Hart kicked his horse lightly. He thought about young Mary Case. During her father's sermons, she often fidgeted, always careful to be sure the tithingman's eyes were averted. Once during one of her father's more impassioned sermons, Mary indulged in a big yawn without even covering her mouth. Other times she gazed out one of the windows, clearly daydreaming. These observations brought a faint smile to Hart's lips. *She finds these long sermons as tedious as the rest of us,* he'd thought to himself.

In some ways, she reminded him of Alice, who was around the same age as Mary when she was killed. His wife's eyes had been as brown as chestnuts, where Mary's were an unusual grey. But recently he detected a new air about her that seemed oddly reminiscent of

Alice when she was in the early stages of pregnancy. This thought brought a flush to Absalom's face. *Could the reverend's daughter be with child?* It was certainly indecent of him to speculate, and her weary appearance could be due merely to ill health…

"Captain Hart! Over here!"

Once again disengaging himself from his thoughts, Hart heard Riff barking several yards away. He clicked to his horse and the roan mare went into a trot until they came to a clearing. One of his men had already dismounted and was staring in horror at a single locust tree with something lashed to it. As he came closer, he saw it was a man, his arrow-riddled body pinned to the tree. His wrists were bound behind him around the tree trunk, and his head listed to one side. He wore a minister's garb and white scarf which now bloomed red with blood.

"That's Parker," a member of the posse muttered in a low voice. "Look what those savages did to him!"

"I reckon there be near thirty arrows or more," another breathed.

The arrows protruded from Parker's corpse like porcupine quills, and Hart appraised the gruesome scene silently while his men spoke of retaliation. Parker's beady eyes peered glassily at nothing while flies buzzed noisily around his blanched face. Hart's head began to throb and he rubbed his eyes with his thumb and forefinger as the men grew more agitated. Finally he ran a hand over his whiskered face and commanded, "We won't engage the Indians on Parker's behalf."

The men gaped at him in disbelief. "What do you mean, Hart?" one demanded. "Look what they done--"

Hart seldom raised his voice, but when he did now, his puzzled deputies balked in surprise.

"We'll retrieve Parker's remains when we can. We haven't the time for it now. The Indian camp can't be too far off."

Riff sniffed the corpse's boots, snarling softly. Then he lifted his leg and urinated on one of Parker's bloodied shins.

The other men protested at this defilement, but Hart merely grasped the beaded belt around Riff's neck and pulled him away without scolding him. *God's honest truth,* Hart thought, *It appears Parker met a justified fate.*

"Mount up," Hart ordered his men.

The small posse quietly obeyed, leaving the slain man impaled against the locust tree.

The sun was beginning to dip beneath the trees, subtly darkening from yellow to orange as the afternoon wore on. The sounds of the forest had stilled, and Hart struggled to control his breathing as his anxiety increased. More than once, the reins slipped from his sweaty palms, but he clenched his jaw and pushed on. Memories of the siege at Cocheco made his scalp prickle as if in anticipation of being lifted from his skull. He knew his party was being watched, and the anticipation of a surprise attack set every fiber of his being as taut as a violin string. With one hand, Hart untied the white neckerchief from his neck and tied it to his musket barrel as the horse plodded on. Then he lifted the musket barrel skyward, his eyes scouring the dense woods for Indians he couldn't see but knew were watching him. Then, without warning, Riff let out an excited bark and darted down the footpath and out of sight, startling Hart and his men almost out of their saddles.

An Algonquin warrior materialized as if from nowhere on the footpath. Hart recognized him by his war paint and tattoos, and knew he was the one who injured Parker and carried him off. A sheathed knife hung from his beaded belt, but otherwise the bare-chested man stood unarmed. His dark eyes fixed on Hart, yet seeming to regard the entire posse at once. Riff was nowhere to be seen.

Hart swallowed over the lump in his throat. He held his musket in one hand, loosely holding the reins in the other in a compliant gesture.

"We mean no harm to you." He hoped he sounded more confident than he felt.

"Captain," whispered James. "What about Parker? We must avenge--"

"We mean no harm," Hart repeated firmly, daring to glance back at his men, who sat frozen in their saddles. When his eyes traveled back to the Indian, he was mildly surprised to see Eames standing next to him. His fringed buckskin breeches and tunic were torn. Like the Indian, he had a knife sheathed and belted to his waist, but was otherwise unarmed. Riff reappeared at his master's side, apparently ecstatic to be reunited with his master, if his wagging tail was any indication.

"Turn back, Hart," Daniel Eames warned ominously. "I don't plan to return to Hereford alive."

Hart exhaled loudly, having expected resistance. "You've got to face justice, Eames."

Eames shook his head. "They'll hang me for sure. Charles here has a dozen warriors trained on you right now. Turn back."

Hart loathed negotiating, especially when the opposition was so difficult to deal with. The terrified cries of Cocheco's victims threatened to echo in his mind as he shifted uncomfortably in his saddle. "If I send these men back, will you speak with me alone?"

He watched Eames and the Indian consider his proposal, and after the Indian nodded, Eames said, "He wants us to return to their village."

"Captain," whispered another of his men, "that would be folly!"

Worse folly would be to get any of my men killed, Hart thought. He looked from Eames to the stony-faced Indian, and finally called for James to approach.

"Take my musket," he said, handing his weapon to the freckled young man. Unarmed, he dismounted and handed the reins to the boy. "Collect Parker's remains and return to Hereford forthwith. If anyone cries out on Parker's behalf, tell them not to assemble until I return. Give me three days' time."

The young deputy looked wide-eyed from Hart to the other men and back again. "But sir--"

"You have your orders," Hart said sternly.

The posse muttered a round of reluctant "yes sirs" before they maneuvered their horses back down the footpath, soon disappearing in the thick forest. When his men had gone, Hart turned to face Eames and the Indian. Holding out his empty arms to them, he felt as vulnerable as a newborn babe. He swallowed, willing the fear to subside.

Eames gave him a crooked grin. "You're a brave man, Hart."

I'm a fool, Hart thought. To Eames, he said, "Lead on, then."

Chapter Twenty-Two

Hart remained silent while Eames and his Indian friend, Charles, led him to the smattering of bark-covered wigwams. He hadn't been in the presence of so many Indians since the night of the siege four years ago, and his stomach clenched with anxiety. The Indians, for their part, eyed him suspiciously. He was introduced to the elderly sachem Eames called Eli, and offered a meal of baked fish and wild roots. Eames acted as interpreter, and the men spoke quietly in a circle after the meal. Against every instinct warning him not to, Hart found himself accepting the invitation to spend the night. As the evening turned to twilight, Hart and Eames were finally left to speak alone, Riff lying contentedly between them, his big snout resting on his paws. Hart watched as Eames withdrew his knife from its beaded sheath and ran it along a whetstone.

"Handsome knife," Hart commented.

Eames nodded. "'Twas mine, then Corwin gave it to some Indian as part of a trade. Charles met up with that Indian, recognized the knife, and learned where I was." His eyes glinted in the twilight as he regarded Hart steadily. "Nothing you say can persuade me to return to Hereford." *Should I tell him my suspicions about Mary?* Hart's face flushed red at the thought. *Nay,* he decided. *'Tis not my place to mention, and it mayn't be true after all.*

"Your heroism at Widow Aker's will lessen your punishment considerably," Hart said, resting his forearms on his knees.

"I went after Riff," Eames explained bluntly.

His honesty is to be admired, Hart thought. "I'll speak on your behalf, and inform the magistrates of Parker's misdeeds." He inhaled the sweet campfire smoke deeply before he continued. "We found his body, Eames. Even when the town knows what Parker did, they'll still want to retaliate against your friends."

"Did you count how many arrows struck him?"

Hart scowled, surprised at this strange question. "Pardon?"

"Twenty-seven," Eames said, answering his own question. "One for every child who succumbed to smallpox after Parker sold them contaminated blankets. Charles recognized him when the others were freeing me."

Hart digested this information with little surprise. "I can mention that to the magistrates also."

"No need. I'm not going back."

Hart exhaled, listening to Eames' knife blade scraping rhythmically against the stone. The noise shredded his nerves while conjuring up still more memories of Cocheco. Finally he blurted, "For Mary's sake, you must return."

Eames eyed him dubiously. Hart swallowed, biting back his suspicions. "She's distraught. They still plan to try her for Dirby's murder, and what with the loss of her sister, she's in a deplorable state."

Eames resumed his sharpening. "She's better off without me."

Hart glanced at Eames' scarred wrists. *From shackles, no doubt*, he thought. He didn't know what darkness lurked in Eames' past, but he knew he'd been exposed to considerable abuse. He thought a moment before he tried another tactic.

"Eames, you have my word, whatever punishment they rule, I will do my best to see that is lessened to the utmost degree."

"I'm not afraid of punishment."

Hart's patience was starting to wane as his exasperation grew. The evening star was now accompanied by a myriad of its fellows and the moon looked like a pearly sickle blade in the night sky. The journey to the Indian camp had taken an entire day and he rubbed his weary eyes.

"'Tis late, but consider my appeal, Eames. I know you're an honorable man."

With that, he rose to his full height and ambled into a nearby wigwam, leaving Eames alone to make his decision.

A minister from neighboring Windsor was summoned to perform the service for Lizzie's funeral. Father was still sorely aggrieved, and he and I clung to each other for support, weeping as the shovelfuls of earth hit the little coffin with dull, solemn thuds. A little stone marked her grave, and it was with the utmost heartache Father and I left our little Lizzie to lie in the cold ground alone.

Hereford's townsfolk were in an uproar over Noah's abduction, moreso than they were of Daniel's escape. On the second day after Daniel's rescue, the townsmen assembled. They discussed the situation heatedly, insisting vengeance on the Indians was indeed called for. Father told me how they ranted on. I wanted to burst forth with the truth about their assistant minister. He—and not Daniel or Charles' band—deserved the severest punishment.

Good men of Hereford took it upon themselves to rebuild Widow Aker's little dwelling. Meanwhile, she lodged with Father and me, sleeping on a pallet near our hearth because she was too feeble to climb the stairs to my loft. I often caught her watching me in a curious way, and finally one afternoon as she and I sat at the hearth with our mending, I set my needle down and demanded to know why she was watching me thus.

"How do you fare, Mary?" Widow Aker asked in her cracking voice.

"Not my best," I admitted. "Heartsick over Lizzie, and I've not yet recovered fully from this fever I contracted--"

Widow Aker lowered her voice. Reverend Case had gone to meet with the townsmen, but was expected to return at any moment. She reached out and palpated Mary's breasts with both hands. Mary winced at the pain and stared at the old woman in outrage. "How dare you?" Mary cried out indignantly.

"Have you missed your courses this month?"

"My courses--?" Mary had forgotten all about keeping track of her cycle. The last one she could remember was two weeks before she met Daniel...

A dreadful realization settled over her. Placing a hand on her abdomen, she looked helplessly at the old midwife. Widow Aker in turn merely worked her toothless jaw and nodded.

"I can smell a breeding woman in the next county," she said in a low voice. "You're in the earliest stages, I reckon."

I can't be with child! Mary's mind screamed. What would Father say? That she ruined herself for the likes of Daniel Eames?

"I can't think," she whispered, glancing anxiously at the closed door, expecting Richard to come in at any moment. "Oh, Widow Aker, what shall I do?"

"I can fix you a concoction to loosen the babe from your womb."

Widow Aker's offer horrified her even more, and Mary clamped her hands over her mouth to keep from screaming aloud. Tears blurred her vision and her stomach roiled. She rocked to and fro, suddenly chilled. *What do I do?* She thought frantically. *I can't have this child, and yet...*

Widow Aker leaned forward and rested a gnarled hand on Mary's knee. Her wrinkled face softened with sorrowful compassion.

If Daniel is returned to me, will he marry me? She somehow doubted he would look favorably upon that prospect. *If he doesn't marry me, it will be the ruin of me! Folks here already look at me with disapproval. And what will Father say? I'm all he has left....*

Before she could voice her fears further, the door opened with a shrill creak. Richard Case walked through the door, his face as pale and solemn as a corpse's. Mary placed both hands protectively over her abdomen, afraid that he'd heard them talking. Instead, he looked from Mary to Widow Aker and back again.

"Daughter, the magistrates insist on going ahead with your hearing," he said hollowly. "They've scheduled it for Tuesday morn. Corwin and Dounton are expected back by then."

"What if the constable doesn't return with the Eames fellow?" Widow Aker asked in her creaking voice.

Richard sighed, stepping closer and placing a trembling hand on Mary's shoulder. "The magistrates say they will have the hearing without him if Corwin produces the witnesses he claims he has."

Mary was still digesting Widow Aker's diagnosis, and her father's news failed to register immediately. She looked helplessly at Widow Aker, who worked her jaw like a cow chewing its cud. Finally she looked at Richard. "What do I do, Father?"

"Pray for deliverance," he replied.

Chapter Twenty-Three

That evening, the militiamen returned with Noah's arrow-riddled body slung awkwardly over Constable Hart's horse. This sent the town into a frenzy of revenge against the Indians. Tuesday morning dawned, just as the militiamen were preparing to retrieve their captain, when Absalom Hart emerged from the wilderness accompanied by Daniel Eames and the ever-faithful Riff. Some of Charles' warriors escorted them by canoe as close to Hereford as they dared, then the two men walked into town just as my hearing was about to begin.

Excited voices announced their arrival and I peered out my loft window. Absalom Hart's deputy approached him, and as I watched, the good constable gave quick instruction to the young man, who hurried off to do Absalom's bidding. My heart beat like a frightened bird in my chest at the sight of Daniel, striding across the courtyard as if he had not a care in the world. Riff was tethered to the whipping post as before, and he whimpered in protest as his master headed towards the meetinghouse with Absalom. Part of me wanted to run into Daniel's arms. Another part wanted to slap his face. Thus were my emotions when Father called softly, "'Tis time, Daughter."

Mary felt as though her legs moved of their own volition, carrying her unwilling torso towards the courtyard. She hesitated until Hart and Daniel had entered the meetinghouse, clutching her father's arm for support. The courtyard crawled like a busy anthill with people making their way to the meetinghouse to watch the proceedings. She kept her eyes on the ground, placing each footfall leadenly.

As they entered the meetinghouse, Mary balked as she almost ran into the burly chest of William Dounton. He leered at her, and she flushed with shame, remembering the humiliating mistreatment she'd endured by his hand.

"We meet again, Miss Mary," he sneered, sending her cringing against her father as her skin crawled. She clenched her eyes shut and depended on Richard to guide her onward while her face continued to flare hotly.

The meetinghouse was filled more than Mary had ever seen it. Seats were few, and many people stood, peering over the shoulders of those in front of them. The warm air was stuffy with so many bodies in the confined space, men fanning themselves with their hats while women used their aprons. Mary made her way to her seat on wobbly legs. Widow Aker regarded her with pity as she worked her toothless jaw silently. Mary dared a quick glance at Daniel and Hart, who'd positioned themselves on the front pew of the men's side. Both men met her eyes briefly; Daniel's cool green eyes regarding her as if nothing were amiss, while Absalom Hart's soulful eyes contained their usual melancholy. George Corwin sat on the same pew, but several feet from Hart and Daniel. His arms were folded tightly against his barrel chest, a scowl of impatience and contempt on his unshaven face.

As Mary approached the chancel, Richard released her arm and headed towards the men's side. Goody Ellis and Goody Hawkins rose from their seats and gently guided her to sit between them. Flanked by the two matrons, Mary felt strangely numb as a voice in her head repeated, *all is lost. All is lost!*

A table had been placed perpendicular to the men's pews. Two magistrates, Joseph Allen and Hiram Stanley, sat with quills poised over a shared ink pot as they glared disdainfully at Mary. A third magistrate and appointed judge, Job Miller, stood behind the pulpit. The grey hairs on his knuckles reminded Mary of a sheep in need of shearing as his bony fingers grasped the rim of the pulpit. He looked prepared to start the preliminary invocation when James returned, a rolled cloth and an extinguished pine knot in his hands. He hastily handed the articles to Hart, who accepted them with a nod, and placed them on the pew beside him. Riff's plaintive whines emanated from the courtyard as Miller rapped the gavel and cleared his throat.

"This hearing will come to order," Miller announced after James seated himself. "It appears we can go forth with Daniel Eames' hearing." Reading from the sheet of paper in front of him, he began, "Theft, escape, abduction and corruption of Miss Mary Case--"

"Your Honors," Absalom Hart said, rising to his feet. "Before we begin, I have information crucial to the matter at hand. May I present it to you?"

After a quick deliberation with his fellow magistrates, Judge Miller said, "You may approach."

The crowd mumbled quietly as Absalom Hart rose with the rolled cloth and the extinguished pine knot in his hands. Hope fluttered briefly in Mary's heart. She wondered how the knowledge of Noah's involvement in Lizzie's death would affect the hearings. She held her breath as Judge Miller stepped down from the pulpit to join the other two magistrates.

Absalom Hart spoke quietly with the magistrates, placing the pine knot on the table and unrolling the cloth to reveal the charcoal sketch of the hoof print he'd drawn on Mary's apron. Mary leaned forward as her hope grew despite an unmoving sense of impending disaster. The magistrates listened intently, regarding Hart with stony faces. Hart spoke lowly, and only a few of his words reached Mary's ears; "Parker—intentional fire—Elizabeth Case." Mary's eyes welled with tears at the sound of her sister's name. She glanced at George Corwin, who apparently heard the case Hart was presenting against his nephew. His face turned into a thundercloud as he rose from his seat.

"How dare you accuse my nephew of such a deed?" Corwin shouted loud enough to silence the murmuring crowd. "A well-respected member of this community, slain so viciously by those heathens!"

"Silence yourself!" Miller snarled, looking up from the hoof print sketch. "The matter of Noah Parker's demise will be dealt with in due course." He deliberated briefly with the other magistrates before returning to the pulpit. After Hart and Corwin were seated, Miller gave the pulpit a swift rap with the gavel and said, "In light of new information, the charges against Daniel Eames will be diminished to a degree we have yet to determine. Constable Hart here has informed me that Eames acted most honorably during the fire at Widow Aker's."

The crowd muttered in agreement. Everyone had either witnessed or heard of Daniel's heroics. Only Corwin rose again, yelling for his nephew's life to be avenged. "That fire was caused by none other than a feeble-minded old hag's carelessness! I demand to know why the militia is not out avenging my nephew's death!"

Mary saw Hart and Daniel exchange a private glance while Miller bellowed, "Corwin, if you make another such outburst, I will have you removed from the premises."

But Corwin continued, his indignant face glistening with sweat. "I have witnesses for the prosecution, Your Honor! I ask to present them now before you declare a final sentencing!"

More excited mumbles from the audience filled the close air and Mary's stomach knotted when Judge Miller consented. A wry smile flitted on Corwin's face for a moment before he gestured to Dounton in the back. All heads turned as Dounton opened the door. Mary heard shuffling and the light, steady tap of a cane against the polished floor before she saw a young man and woman walk up the aisle with an older woman between them. The young man was short and stockily built. Dirt filled deep creases in his calloused hands. The young woman's eyebrows were parted with a deep vertical cleft and the corners of her mouth turned down sourly. The older woman took small, careful steps. A gnarled hand gripped the cane as she made her way slowly up the aisle. Her other hand gripped the corner of her apron, which she kept pressed to her mouth. As she grew closer, Mary inhaled sharply. The older woman had Daniel's eyes. But where his were cool and glinting, hers were hooded in pain and sorrow. *That's Daniel's mother!* Mary realized. *She who endured the horrors of the witch dungeon!*

Time seemed to crawl as the three witnesses approached the

pulpit. Corwin smiled triumphantly as Dounton joined him, both looking smug. Mary shot a quick glance at Daniel, whose face had blanched. He shed his nonchalant attitude like a cloak and leaped to his feet. With a savage cry, he lunged at Corwin.

"You had no right to bring them here!" he yelled.

The gavel rapped sharply and Miller bellowed, "Order! Hart, contain him. Corwin, please have your witnesses introduce themselves."

As Absalom Hart gently but firmly placed himself between Daniel and Corwin, Corwin smirked evilly. The stocky young man removed his hat and gave Daniel a quick look before saying, "Your Honor, I'm John Eames, brother of Daniel."

The magistrates scribbled the name down furiously while the older woman took a step forward, her cane tapping softly. "Your Honor, I'm Rebecca Eames, his mother."

Mary felt somewhat awestruck. Daniel had made it sound as though his mother were some wronged angelic being, and she was intrigued by the small, slight woman whose rasping voice bespoke of long suffering and misery. Mary fixed her eyes on Rebecca Eames, wishing she could speak to the woman privately. As her mind entertained that thought, the dour-faced woman stepped up.

"Your Honor," she said, her voice tight and hateful. "I'm Lydia Eames. Daniel's wife."

Chapter Twenty-Four

Mary's throat went dry and an icy sweat glazed her skin as she looked at the indignant woman. *Daniel's wife!* The word echoed in her head as the crowd gasped in excited horror. Her ears began to ring, and were it not for Goodwives Ellis and Hawkins grasping her shoulders, she would have fallen off the pew.

Such hateful looks passed between Daniel and Lydia that Mary felt their contempt for each other. Her stomach clenched violently. She pressed her stained apron to her mouth, willing herself not to be sick.

Judge Miller scowled at Daniel, who glowered murderously at Corwin and Dounton. "Are you still lawfully married to this woman?"

Daniel stood his eyes still ablaze with defiance. "Aye."

"And during the time Mary Case was in your company, did you have relations with her?"

Daniel kept his eyes straight ahead. "Aye."

Mary felt every eye shift onto her as the crowd gasped excitedly. Her face again flushed and she stared at her hands in her lap, wishing she could disappear. Goody Ellis placed a sympathetic hand over Mary's, but Mary was numb to it. A confusing myriad of emotions swirled within her heart and mind. Of them all, a numbing fear rose to the top like cream in a bucket of standing milk.

"Mary Case, you will rise."

Judge Miller's summoning sounded as though he were speaking to her underwater. She shook her head to clear her ears of the ringing inside them, but to no avail. She felt both Goody Ellis and Goody

Hawkins grasp her by each elbow and gently lift her to her feet. Mary's legs felt like limp rags as she shuffled towards the waiting magistrates. Daniel stood just two feet away, but she couldn't bear to look at him. She kept her eyes glued to the floor, and when her escorts released her arm to return to their seats, she whispered urgently, "Don't leave me!"

She felt a slight comfort as both women retained their holds, and felt as if she would collapse without their support.

"Mary Case," Miller asked gravely, "do you admit to having fornicated with Daniel Eames, a married man?"

Mary's mouth felt dry as she opened it to speak, but no sound came out. *I did not know he was a married man!* She wanted to shout in defense. She continued to stare at the floor, nodding her head in confirmation.

"Give 'aye' or 'nay,' for the record!" Miller demanded. "speak up, woman!"

"Aye," she finally croaked.

Miller and his fellow magistrates deliberated for a moment while Mary stood there, feeling like a lamb facing the butcher's block. She heard the crowd murmuring behind her and willed her stomach to settle. Then Miller rapped the gavel, causing her to jump. Goody Ellis and Goody Hawkins tightened their holds on her as she began to sway unsteadily.

Judge Miller glowered from the pulpit at both Daniel and Mary. "It appears we have substantial evidence to try you both. Daniel Eames' trial will begin early Thursday morn. Mary Case's will follow immediately after." He rapped the lectern with finality. "These hearings are adjourned. Constable, escort Daniel Eames to the jailhouse."

Mary felt like she'd collapse were it not for the support Goody Ellis and Goody Hawkins provided. She continued to stare at the floor as if she were peering at it through a knothole; nothing else existed.

"Mary--" Daniel's voice penetrated the fogginess in her brain.

"You've done quite enough, you miscreant," Goody Ellis snapped, tightening her grip on Mary's elbow. "To bring a decent young maid to such degradation!" Goody Ellis softened her voice and whispered into Mary's ear, "Anne and I will sit with you until the meetinghouse has cleared. We won't let that scoundrel *near* you." Mary felt Goody Ellis place a commanding arm over her shoulders and guide her back to the front pew.

"I demand justice for the slaying of my nephew!" Corwin continued to rant as Mary sat wearily. She kept her eyes on the floor, hearing the mumbling crowd quietly exit the meetinghouse. Her face felt as though she were sitting in front of a blazing hearth while the rest of her felt cold and sick. Among the chorus of retreating footsteps, she heard the light, steady tap of Rebecca Eames' cane. It faded to nothingness and the meetinghouse fell deathly silent.

A pair of men's boots stepped into her narrow line of vision, and she heard her father's soft baritone through the ringing in her ears.

"Daughter, I'll escort you home."

"Has—has Daniel left yet?"

"Aye," Richard replied.

"And his…family?"

"That they have."

Mary blinked away tears and finally glanced up at her father while the goodwives sat like coifed bookends on either side of her. "Father, what shall I do?"

He exhaled, his thin chest heaving beneath his doublet. *If his advice is to pray, I'll scream,* Mary thought desperately. Instead, he remained silent as he offered a quivering hand to her. She took it, mildly surprised at how cold and limp it felt. *He's no stronger than I.* A growing sense of helplessness mushroomed inside her at this sudden realization.

With the goodwives' assistance, Mary rose on quaking legs. Turning to face the door, she was relieved to see that the meetinghouse was indeed empty. Her chest felt tight and she yearned to fill her lungs with fresh air. On her father's arm and with the goodwives in their wake, Mary walked as if in a miserable dream out of the meetinghouse and into the warm mid-September air.

A few people milled about in the courtyard, throwing curious glances at Mary as she emerged. She felt as vulnerable as if she were standing naked before them, and her face flared hot. Riff yipped in recognition, straining at his tether. His big eyes glimmered beseechingly at her. He glanced forlornly at the jailhouse, then back at her. His sad whine tore at her heart.

"Father," she whispered, "Pray, let me alone a minute." To Goody Ellis and Goody Hawkins, she said, "Thank you both for your support."

Goody Ellis expelled an indignant *hmph* at this dismissal. "As you wish," she replied, giving Goody Hawkins a quick nod. Mary waited until both women had crossed the courtyard and disappeared before looking at her father. She clasped his trembling hand in both of hers and said, "I just need a moment."

Richard seemed reluctant to release her hand. "Don't be long." He gave her hand a final squeeze and ambled towards the rectory like a man of advanced age.

Alone in the courtyard, Mary approached Riff, whose tail wagged slowly in gratitude. She knelt beside him, stroking his big head and scratching his shaggy neck. He lapped at her face as a flood of tears poured from her eyes. She embraced his shoulders and sobbed, "Oh, Riff, what am I to do?"

Riff looked meaningfully at the jailhouse and whimpered again. "You want to be with your master, don't you?" she murmured. "But alas, I can't bring you to him. I can't bear the sight of Daniel right now." Riff lowered his head and nudged her abdomen, sniffing delicately. *He senses the child within,* she thought suddenly. Glancing anxiously at the jailhouse, she fingered the beaded belt thoughtfully, remembering the back-breaking work forced upon her by Hurit. But then she recalled the nights with Daniel, and how safe she felt in his arms. Her heart ached, arguing once again with her mind. *I must face him,* she thought. *He needs to know about the babe I carry.*

Her hands seemed to untie Riff of their own volition, and the dog fidgeted in anticipation when she rose from her knees. "Come then, you good boy," she said. "Only with your presence can I face him."

He trotted beside her as she walked woodenly towards the jailhouse. *I'll just tell him of my condition,* she told herself, unsure of what she hoped would be his reaction. Would he be glad? Angry? Dispassionate?

Loud voices emanated from the jailhouse windows, stopping her in her tracks. Riff looked up at her questioningly. He clearly yearned to be reunited with Daniel, but Mary paused, gripping the belt firmly.

"I for one am not surprised at the shame you brought upon your family," Lydia Eames was shouting. "All the times you abandoned us in the past, I knew it would come to this!"

"Lydia--" Daniel began.

"Nothing, *nothing* you say can repair the damage you've done!" Lydia continued.

Mary was a mere two yards from the jailhouse now, and she crept closer, keeping a firm grip on Riff's belt. Kneeling behind the ash barrel below the window, she drew a restless Riff close to her. She pressed against the clapboards, Lydia Eames' words tumbling over her like a pot of boiling oil.

"Brother," John Eames' voice was soft-spoken and measured. "Come home with us."

"I don't want him to return with us," Lydia snapped viciously. "Unless he's prepared to cut me loose with a divorcement."

Mary heard quiet, steady sobs, and assumed they came from Daniel's mother. She swallowed, and breathed silently through her mouth, her arms around Riff as he strained to join his family. *Please be still and quiet!* Mary beseeched the dog silently. She suddenly felt trapped, and pressed closer against the ash barrel.

"Lydia," Daniel began again, "I know I've never been a decent husband to you. 'Tis why I left for good this last time. I felt it was for the best."

"'*For the best*'?" the wronged woman screeched. "When is it ever *for the best* to abandon your wife and children, who depend on you?"

Children. Daniel and his wife have children. This revelation surprised Mary. It hadn't occurred to her that Daniel could already be a father. She placed a hand on her abdomen and fought back a wave of nausea.

"My absence will make Solomon and Jethro harder men," Daniel argued defensively.

"Indeed!" Lydia's voice rose in pitch, pricking Mary's ears. "Hard and cold, willing to abandon wives of their own! Well, let them hang you or flog you for your misdeeds. I care not what happens to your worthless hide!"

Angry footfalls clipped along the floor and onto the stoop. Riff struggled against Mary's grip and ran excitedly to the jailhouse door.

"Riff!" Mary heard Lydia mutter. "How did you get loose? I thought they had you tied…"

Daniel's brother and mother continued to speak to him in low tones, then exclaimed as Riff bounded in. Mary's heart froze as she heard the same footfalls growing closer. Daniel's wrathful wife was approaching! She cringed between the barrel and the jailhouse, petrified. Drawing her knees up to her chin, she closed her eyes and willed herself to disappear.

"Behold the cowardly slut!" Lydia Eames declared in a voice dripping with animosity. "Eavesdropping on a private conversation! Nefarious wretch!"

Before she could think, Mary was seized by the shoulders by Lydia's talon-like hands. The enraged woman yanked Mary to her feet and shook her until her teeth rattled in her head. Stunned, Mary drew her arms protectively over her abdomen and suffered the attack defenselessly.

"Lydia! Lydia, stop!" a man's voice demanded, and eventually the angry hands were peeled away from her shoulders by Daniel's brother. Mary trembled uncontrollably and buried her face in her apron. She couldn't bear to look at anyone, least of all Daniel's wife. She slumped against the ash barrel and sobbed.

A soft, rhythmic tapping sound grew closer, then stopped.

Mary felt a warm, gentle hand settle on her shoulder as if a small bird had landed there. "John, pray, return Lydia to the tavern. I'd like to have a private word with this young maid."

Mary held her breath, cutting off her sobs abruptly. *What could Daniel's mother have to say to me?* She wondered in trepidation.

"But Mother--"

"John." Rebecca Eames said with finality. "First, Lydia, you will apologize for your behavior."

"*Mother Eames!*" Lydia cried indignantly. "She's fornicated with Daniel and--"

"Apologize, Daughter."

Still cringing against the ash barrel, Mary heard Lydia mutter an insincere apology before stomping off.

"Take Riff along and get him a hambone." Rebecca directed. Mary marveled at the power the small matron wielded. She listened intently as John retreated, Riff panting softly. Mary kept her head buried in her arms until she felt Rebecca's hands on her shoulders, gently pulling her upright. Mary turned to face the little woman she'd grown to idolize, and sucked in her breath. The woman's eyes were so like Daniel's it pained her. But where Daniel's glinted with a cold carelessness, hers were softened by compassion and sorrow.

"Goodwife Eames--" Mary began, clasping her hands to her bosom.

"Widow," Rebecca corrected her.

Mary swallowed. "Widow Eames, please forgive me. I didn't know--"

Rebecca plucked Mary's left hand from her bosom while her other hand clutched the cane. "Walk me to the tavern. 'Tis difficult for me to walk unaided."

Mary obeyed, again surprised at how warm the woman's hand was. Rebecca took tiny steps, and Mary remembered Daniel mentioning she'd lost all her toes due to frostbite during her incarceration. Looking down at Widow Eames' scuffed shoes, she shivered at the recollection. Matching her steps to Rebecca's, she tried again to apologize.

"I didn't know Daniel was--"

"Pray, allow me to share something with you I've not even told my children."

Mary closed her mouth, her eyes on the woman's pallid face. Her nose was similar to Daniel's, but smaller and more delicate. Rebecca glanced up at Mary. Her eyes, as green and turbulent as a stormy sea, reflected hard-won wisdom and sorrowful regret.

"When I was in my fifteenth year," Rebecca continued, her voice low. "I was bonded out to a William Cogswell in Ipswich. He and his wife had five small children, all of whom were left in my charge. I slept under the eaves in their garret."

Why is she sharing this with me, something so personal? Mary wondered as Rebecca's cane tapped lightly against the packed earth.

"One morning, Goodwife Cogswell sent me to the stream to rinse out the baby's soiled clouts." Mary held her breath in anticipation as Rebecca wet her thin lips before she continued. "Goodman Cogswell came upon me, and thus I learned the way of men."

Mary's heart chilled in her chest at this confession. Speechless, she glanced around, but the street was vacant except for a man pushing a wheelbarrow down the opposite side. She looked back at Rebecca, who continued to stare straight ahead, her small face appearing to darken with the horrid memory. Mary swallowed uncomfortably. "Widow Eames, I don't think I should be hearing--"

"'Tis an unforgettable occasion when a girl loses her maidenhood," Rebecca went on. "'Twas fortunate I didn't become with child, and it's my sincerest hope your babe was not conceived through brutality."

Mary stopped in the middle of the street, still gripping Widow Eames' hand. "How did you know?"

The green eyes met hers with bittersweet compassion. "I saw how you shielded your belly from Lydia's rage just now. Does Daniel know?"

"Nay. Only Widow Aker, the midwife, knows," Mary replied. "I was on my way to tell Daniel when I heard his wife…."

Rebecca nodded. "Lydia's been bitter for a long time. She was wrong to attack you so viciously."

"I didn't know he was married," Mary insisted. "I thought he… he loved me."

She felt Rebecca squeeze her hand. "My son is not a bad man. He's always suffered from wanderlust, and being tied down to a farm and family was never his calling. He and Lydia were ill-matched from the start, and neither of them is happy with the other."

Mary felt as though some invisible bond had grown between her and Daniel's mother. She was sorry to see the tavern looming just down the street, and John Eames striding purposefully towards them on short, stocky legs. He eyed Mary questioningly, but without hostility as he approached them and took his mother's hand from Mary.

"I thank you for walking my mother back," he said softly, meeting Mary's eyes briefly.

Mary released Rebecca's hand reluctantly. Their private conversation worked like a balm on her spirit, and she felt better than she had in long time. "Widow Eames," she blurted, "May we speak again sometime?"

Rebecca Eames gave a slight smile, but it quickly died on her lips. "We need to return to Boxford as soon as the sentence is carried out. But mayhap we'll meet again…before that."

As Daniel's mother turned away from her, Mary felt as if a piece of her soul had merged with that of the Widow Eames', and was being stretched taut, ready to snap free, never to return.

Chapter Twenty-five

The warmth of Rebecca's touch still lingered on Mary's hand as she turned to retrace her steps. She smiled, hoping to be in the older woman's calming presence again soon. As much as Daniel's wife oozed animosity and resentment, his mother exuded forgiveness and compassion. *What a remarkable woman*, Mary found herself thinking. *To show such grace to me, despite all she has been through!*

A young boy rolling a hoop ran past Mary, jarring her from her reverie as he brushed past her cloak. "Pardon, lady," he called over his shoulder without much conviction. Glancing up from the dusty road, Mary recognized the Widow Aker's stooped figure ambling towards her, her toothless jaw grinding silently.

"Widow Aker, where are you going?" Mary asked as they met.

"The men have finished repairs on my house," Widow Aker replied. "Enough that it's habitable, I'm told. I'm heading back there now."

"Will I see you ….at my trial on the morrow?" Mary asked.

"Nay. Methinks I need a good day or two of solitude, for my own soul's healing."

Mary nodded, disappointment settling over her like an ache. She was hoping to see as many friendly faces at her trial as possible. She realized Widow Aker was carrying no possessions, and Mary knew she'd lost everything in the fire. "You haven't even a pallet to sleep on. May I bring you a quilt at least?"

The old woman's milky eyes crinkled as she smiled. "That would be kind of you, dear. And my heart is gladdened you've forgiven me for Lizzie…"

As always, the mention of Lizzie brought fresh tears to Mary's eyes. A lump formed in her throat as she took the midwife's hands and assured her, "Her passing was the doing of none other than that wretch Noah Parker."

"I fear he's earned martyrdom in the eyes of some folk," Widow Aker said, glancing over her shoulder. "Men are congregating in the courtyard as we speak."

A cold hand of dread seized Mary and she drew her cloak tighter around herself. "What do you mean, Widow Aker?"

The old woman scowled. "Those accursed troublemakers from Salem are rousing the men of Hereford to seek revenge for Reverend Parker's death. They seek to kill them savages that riddled his body with arrows. Pray, go see for yourself. I'm on my way to set up my house." She patted Mary's cheek with her dry, thin-skinned hand. "God be with you, Mary."

"And with you," Mary replied quietly as she followed the retreating woman with her eyes. Widow Aker's words disturbed her, and she grew more concerned as she hurried towards the courtyard.

That damnable Corwin and despicable Dounton! She thought as she quickened her pace. For all the hard work they'd forced upon her, the Indians had treated her with considerably more respect and dignity than those two had. When she looked back on those days at the Indian camp, it was almost with fondness, and she feared for Charles, Eli and their people. She even felt concern for sour-faced Hurit, and found herself considering who the real savages were as she neared the meetinghouse.

As she grew closer, she heard angry men's voices and saw a cluster of militiamen growing more agitated while they listened to a speaker in their midst. She recognized the voice as Corwin's, and pressed herself against the clapboards of the meetinghouse. She hoped they hadn't seen her, and her stomach churned at the sound of Corwin's voice, inciting the other men to violence.

"My nephew's death needs to be avenged!" Corwin bellowed. "You saw what those demon savages did to him, and I'll not rest until every one of those devils are slaughtered!"

"Reverend Parker was a good man," someone agreed. "He baptized my twin sons just a month ago."

"I'm certain there are those among you with your own grievances against the heathen," Corwin encouraged.

"They steal!" offered another man. "Robertson here caught them burgling his smokehouse just last week."

"Aye," Robertson agreed. "Snagged two whole hams and a side of venison."

"So who's with me?" Corwin demanded. "Who's willing to avenge my nephew, and the other wrongs done to this blessed community?"

They mean to attack Charles and his folk, Mary realized, pressing a trembling hand to her mouth. A unified cry went up, and Mary glanced anxiously at the jailhouse. Surely Daniel and Constable Hart had heard these threats of violence. Would anyone be able to warn Charles of the impending attack? Although she'd been forced to work hard while living among the Indians, she'd grown to respect them, and she didn't want to see harm come to them, especially if it were to avenge the likes of Noah Parker.

She remained rooted to the spot as she heard the men disperse, their minds clearly set on bloodshed. Even after their agitated voices and heavy footfalls died away, she clung to the side of the meeting-house, unsure what to do.

Two large hands settled on her shoulders. Startled, she jumped and almost cried out.

"Mary," Constable Hart said in a low voice, turning her around to face him. She looked up into his melancholy face. "'Tis not safe for you to be wandering about alone."

"Oh, Absalom!" She whispered, clasping both hands over her racing heart. "Did you hear what those men mean to do?"

"Aye," he replied. "My own militia won't listen to me; that dog Corwin has them so bent on vengeance. Allow me to escort you back to the rectory."

"I…I wanted to visit Daniel," she said, her hands falling to her abdomen.

Mary saw Hart's eyes lower briefly, then rise again as his face flushed slightly. *Is my condition already so obvious?* Mary wondered as her own face reddened.

"Better that you go on to the rectory," he insisted, releasing her shoulders. "Your father is wondering about you, no doubt."

She placed both hands on his arm imploringly. "Please, Absalom. I only want to speak to Daniel for a moment."

Hart blew out a breath and regarded Mary with a look of such understanding she was sure he knew she was with child. "Come along then," he said, offering his arm.

James, the only member of Hart's militia who'd stayed behind, was sitting on a stool near the cell door when Hart and Mary entered the jailhouse. An upturned bucket with several playing cards on it sat before James' knobby knees. Daniel sat on his emptied water bucket, hands protruding through the bars, holding five cards.

"You lose, Jimmy," Daniel grinned, revealing a winning hand and splaying the cards on the bucket. "That's near twelve pence you owe me."

James shook his head and threw his worthless cards down. He was about to speak when he realized Hart and Mary had entered. His face paled, then flushed as he rose from his seat, upsetting the bucket. The entire deck of cards scattered to the floor as he looked shamefacedly at the constable.

"Sir, I was just--"

"Excuse us for a moment, James," Hart interrupted, holding the door open so the young man could leave. "But first, pick those up."

"Yes, sir."

The embarrassed young man snatched up the scattered deck. He looked nervously at the jail's small hearth where orange embers winked.

"You needn't burn them," Hart said. "Tuck them into your vestments and leave us."

James looked relieved and stuffed the deck into his shirt. Then he plucked his hat from its peg on the wall, slapped it on his head and touched the brim briefly at Mary before darting out of the jailhouse. Owning a deck of cards was forbidden in Hereford, and if the magistrates heard James had been gambling— especially while on duty--he would find himself in the stocks.

Mary kept her eyes on the floorboards as Hart closed the door behind the young deputy. His gentle touch on her elbow propelled her forward until the bottom rungs of the cell came into view. She heard Daniel from within the cell rise to his feet.

"I can leave you two alone, but only for a moment," Hart said in his low voice.

Mary suddenly felt the urge to ask him to stay. She wasn't sure if she could bear speaking to Daniel alone. She remained as stationary as a fence post as she heard Hart's foot falls across the floor. The door opened, then closed softly and for the first time in a long time, she was alone with Daniel.

"Mary, look at me."

If I look at him, I'm liable to scream. Or weep. Or both, she thought. Slowly her eyes traveled up his lean leather-clad body. Her heart warmed at the recollection of their lovemaking. But when her gaze reached his eyes, the warmth was replaced by the cold memory of betrayal. His long fingers grasped the bars as he regarded her in cool silence, the red T glaring prominently on his hand.

"You have a wife and didn't tell me," she said, the word *wife* falling flat and bitter on her tongue.

His glinting green eyes looked apologetic for a moment, and his gaze made her heart hurt. "'Twas my feeling Lydia and the boys would be better off without me."

"Aye. I heard you speaking earlier." She inhaled deeply, prepared to tell him, but instead she said, "Your mother spoke most kindly to me."

At the mention of his mother, Daniel's featured softened. "My mother's a kind woman."

Mary nodded in agreement, debating whether she should tell him about the baby. Instead, she asked with little hope, "Would you not consider a divorcement from Lydia, so that you might be free to wed again?"

Something disturbing darkened his eyes, sending a cold shiver through Mary. "A wife and children were never what I sought in life. I'll not make that mistake again, and I doubt any man would want a scold like Lydia, so there's no sense in a formal divorcement."

Her shoulders sagged. *Then hearing about this child I carry won't be a joy to him*, she thought sullenly. "But what of your feelings for me?"

His Adam's apple bobbed in his throat and his mouth set in a grim line. "We had our time together, and now it appears it's passed."

His words pierced her heart as viciously as a wolf's fangs. *He never loved me*, she realized, tears threatening to spill down her cheeks. Anger flickered, growing into a full blaze within her as the next thought formed. *He doesn't deserve to know about this child!* She met his gaze so steadily his eyebrows rose briefly in surprise.

"Then I've nothing more to say to you," she said coldly. She attempted to harden her features, but hot tears welled in her eyes and slid down her cheeks. "I'll not visit you again."

The last word broke into a sob and she spun away to flee the jailhouse. She hadn't heard the door open, and blinded by tears, she crashed into Constable Hart's solid chest. His hands grasped her shoulders and he pulled her from him, gazing into her tear-streaked face with concern.

"What's this, Mary?" he asked, allowing her to crumple against him again. "Did you tell--?"

Mary pulled away and looked up at Hart, shaking her head almost undetectably. To emphasize her need for secrecy, she placed an index finger across her lips. "I've said all I need to say to him, Absalom," she said. "Pray, escort me to the rectory now."

She watched Hart's brooding eyes flit to Daniel, then back to her before he nodded. "Come then," he said. The young deputy emerged from behind Hart, evidently confused about the situation. Hart turned to him and said, "James, I'll return shortly. I suggest you not break out that deck of cards again."

The boy's face grew pink, and he mumbled a reply Mary didn't hear as Hart placed an arm around her shoulders and propelled her out of the jailhouse.

Sniffling and dabbing at her runny nose with her apron, Mary heard Hart close the door softly behind them. Then he offered his arm and she accepted it gratefully as they walked slowly across the courtyard. She swallowed over the lump and her voice was a cracked whisper when she spoke.

"When did you suspect I…that I…"

Hart cleared his throat. They were alone in the courtyard, but he kept his voice low. "I've seen that…*luminance*…before. It radiates from within like a candle."

Mary knew virtually nothing about Hart's past, and intuitively she sensed something tragic had occurred. "What happened?"

Hart's footfalls were slow and heavy. "Near four years ago in New Hampshire. Indians attacked. Those they didn't kill outright, they took captive to Canada."

"Did they—did they seize your wife?"

His jaw tightened and his Adam's apple bobbed in his throat before he replied. "Nay. She was among those they killed. She'd just told me she was with child before the massacre."

Hart stopped and looked at her. His eyes held so much sadness her heart broke for him. "Her name was Alice."

To hear that my good friend had endured such undeserved heartache eclipsed my current miseries and O how I felt for Constable Hart! I wanted to know more, but I knew it pained him deeply to speak of it, so we traversed the remaining distance in silence, both immersed in our own sorrows.

Chapter Twenty-Six

The next day was Lecture Day, and the face that greeted Mary in the looking glass that morning looked gaunt. She'd slept little, and her eyes appeared dark and sunken. Her shorn hair barely touched her shoulders and had become matted. When she ran a brush through it, she was alarmed to find an abundance of follicles clinging to the bristles. She felt her scalp, and both horror and dismay chilled her as she realized her hair was falling out. *As my life falls apart, so does my physical self,* she thought glumly. After she tied her coif strings around her chin, she freed the mass of hair from the brush. Balled up in her hand, it was nearly the size of a large rat, and she tossed it into the hearth flames as she entered the hall. She was reminded of the last time she burned her hair, the foul smell sickening her stomach. Like then, the act of sacrificing hair ended one chapter of her life as another began.

Mary's father busied himself putting the finishing touches on his lecture, never looking directly at Mary. She assumed he suspected her condition as well, and they ate their breakfast pottage in uncomfortable silence before joining the assembled townspeople in the courtyard.

The few mouthfuls Mary had been able to swallow sat in a heavy mass in her stomach as she took her customary place among the townswomen, draped in her woolen cloak. The September sun shone brightly in the Eastern sky, but Mary felt as cold and empty as a shattered egg shell. The town magistrates congregated together in the shade of a young poplar tree which grew on a small knoll next to the meetinghouse. This gave them the appearance of rising above the plain folk who gathered in the courtyard below. *Tomorrow they will determine my fate,* Mary thought dully. *Mine, and Daniel's.*

Just as she shook the thought of Daniel from her mind, Mary heard the soft, rhythmic tapping of a cane on bare earth. She glanced up and recognized the Eames family making their way slowly across the courtyard. Riff lumbered obediently next to John Eames, who'd tied a leash around the beaded belt Mary had placed around the dog's shaggy neck. Riff acknowledged her with a gentle tail wag and a soft whine before he sat on his haunches between John and Rebecca. She considered how faithful the dog was to his family, and realized sadly she herself had never been the object of such devotion.

Mary again felt the unexplainable connection she'd sensed when she was in Rebecca's presence, and longed to stand next to the older woman. Instead, she was again flanked by Goodwives Ellis and Hawkins, who apparently considered Mary their charge whenever she was out in public. Mary expected to see Daniel in the pillory. Instead, Samson Fields, the hot-tempered carpenter, was locked in the device. A cloth with the word *Drunkard* scrawled on it dangled from a string placed over his neck. The florid-faced man glared defiantly at his neighbors. He shouted obscenities and demanded to be released, but to no avail. His hat had fallen to the ground and his red, bulbous nose was webbed with broken blood vessels.

Mayhap the magistrates are saving Daniel for his trial tomorrow, she thought dully, glad of his absence.

As her father took his place with Bible in hand, he began the day's lecture with a prayer. All eyes closed and heads bowed, except for Mary's. She knew by her father's tone his heart was not in his sermon as she stood as stiff and unfeeling as a fence post, her unfocused mind flitting like a butterfly from one thought to the next. Her gaze remained on Daniel's mother, and she was compelled to approach the Widow Eames. The small woman bowed her head, both hands stacked on the top of her cane. Her sallow, pock-marked face retained a serene kind of beauty, and although her narrow shoulders sloped considerably, there was a fearlessness about Rebecca Eames. *Surely, if she endured the horrors Daniel spoke of,* Mary thought with admiration, *she's stronger than anyone here, man or woman!* She silently willed the older woman to look at her, but Rebecca's eyes remained closed while her son John and Daniel's wife stood next to her. Lydia Eames seemed to sense Mary's steady gaze, and after a moment she raised her head and sent Mary a deadly glare that made her shiver and avert her eyes.

As the lecture droned on to its dispassionate benediction, the congregation gave a collective sigh and Mary rolled her stiff shoulders as discreetly as she could beneath her cloak. Samson Fields' punishment was to spend the rest of the afternoon in the pillory while youngsters were encouraged to throw rotten food at him. John Eames took his mother's arm, his face reddening as he glanced quickly at Mary then back again. He seemed so different from Daniel. They didn't resemble each other physically. Where Daniel was red-haired and lanky, John had a shorter, stockier build and dark hair beneath his felt hat. Mary watched Rebecca longingly as John and Lydia escorted her across the courtyard. *Please, spare a moment and have a word with me!* She wanted to cry out. *Your words—nay, your very presence is such a comfort to me, Widow Eames!*

"Come along, love," Goody Ellis was saying, pulling gently on Mary's elbow. "'Tis time for your midday meal. Look—your father has already gone to the rectory."

"Leave me be," Mary snapped, shaking off Goody Ellis' touch with irritation. "I don't require a chaperone!"

Goody Ellis huffed and summoned Goody Hawkins. "Come then, Anne. Good day, Mary."

The two matrons raised their chins in indignation and left Mary standing in the courtyard, where she watched Rebecca Eames make slow progress towards the dusty lane. She watched until the Eames family disappeared around a corner. Realizing she was now alone in the courtyard except for Samson Fields, whose bare hands and hatless head poked from the pillory. He regarded her with bloodshot eyes squinted almost shut against the bright sun.

"Fetch me some ale, girl!" he bellowed. "I'll die of thirst locked in this contraption!"

When Mary didn't respond, he demanded, "At the very least, return my hat to my head! I feel the sun baking my very scalp."

Immersed in her own dark emotions, Mary barely registered his pleas. She glanced briefly at the jailhouse before she turned away and joined her father in the rectory.

The remainder of that day lingered miserably, and yet each passing minute drew my trial dangerously closer to the present. I ate little and slept less, anticipating the morrow with such dread I couldn't even focus on my sewing. I only managed to prick my finger, and as the blood beaded on my fingertip, I wondered how much more I would shed when I received my punishment.

Chapter Twenty-Seven

The morning of Mary's and Daniel's trial dawned bleak and overcast, mirroring Mary's hopeless mood. She had grown so thin her ribs rubbed painfully against her stays, and she took care not to twist against the firm fabric. Her aching breasts were swelling with milk, dampening the front of her shift and leaving a sour odor. Everything inside her had grown numb as she stared into her bowl of pottage. She couldn't bring herself to eat one spoonful, and she felt that her entire being was as hollow as her empty stomach.

"Eat something, Daughter," Reverend Case encouraged, having finished his own meager bowlful. "You've grown so thin."

She looked up from her bowl and bit her bottom lip. His face wore an expression of deep concern and dismay. Did he suspect she was with child? *If Father doesn't suspect already, he will find out soon enough of my condition,* she thought glumly.

The meetinghouse bell chimed, and Mary rose from the board feeling like a lamb being led to slaughter. Silently she draped her woolen cloak over her shoulders and followed her father. She smelled rain approaching and prayed the cloudy heavens would release a torrent to rival the Deluge. *Then I could mercilessly drown and be done with this misery,* she told herself.

A sharp bark drew her attention to the whipping post, where Riff had again been tied. *So Daniel's family has already arrived,* Mary thought as she passed by him. He gave her an imploring look, and she wanted to comfort the unhappy dog, but her father's hand on her back propelled her forwards.

"Courage, Daughter," was all he managed to say before opening the meetinghouse door for her. Behind them, Riff released a plaintive howl.

Her shift clung uncomfortably to her body as she entered the meetinghouse. Eyes lowered, she walked past the gauntlet of onlookers and took her seat. Once again she was bookended by Goodwives Ellis and Hawkins, but they seemed coolly detached and less accommodating than before. Mary pulled the brim of her cap further so she wouldn't see them in her peripheral vision and was sure to cocoon herself in her cloak to conceal the conspicuous milk stains on her shift. Across from her sat Daniel, flanked by Hart and young James. She narrowed her field of vision to a small spot in the center of the polished oak floor. Everything seemed to take on an otherworldly effect as she stared intently at that one spot. Mumbling voices dissolved into insect-like buzzing and despite being in a room filled to capacity, Mary had never felt more alone.

Judge Miller and his fellow magistrates strode into the meetinghouse with rigid postures. Goodwives Ellis and Hawkins rose, each seizing an elbow, and pulled Mary to a standing position as everyone stood until Judge Miller took his place behind the lectern and the preliminary formalities began. With one sharp rap of the gavel, Miller stated, "We'll have the defendant Eames approach."

Mary heard Daniel rise, and by the shuffling of his steps she assumed they had fettered his ankles. His footfalls were accompanied by those of two other men, and she glanced up quickly to see Daniel was flanked by both Hart and the young deputy James. Rain pattered lightly, then more heavily, on the meetinghouse roof and Mary shivered despite the muggy heat.

"Daniel Eames," Miller intoned gravely, "have you anything to say in your defense?"

"Your Honor," she heard Absalom Hart say in his steady voice, "May I remind the court of this man's noble actions in retrieving young Elizabeth Case from the fire, which was deliberately set by the late Reverend Noah Parker?"

At the mention of her sister's name, Mary looked up from the floor. Daniel stood with wrists bound, but his jaw was set and his eyes glared forward in sheer defiance. If he saw her in his peripheral vision, he made no indication. His refusal to look at her stabbed her heart. Next to him, Absalom Hart met her eyes briefly before returning to Judge Miller.

The crowd murmured excitedly at this and some voices rose up in protest. "Who besmirches the good name of our belated Reverend Parker?" a man demanded.

Miller rapped his gavel sharply in an attempt to regain order. When the angry chatter subsided, he continued.

"We have been shown proof of the late Reverend Parker's actions, but the savages have seen fit to deliver his death sentence, and he is no longer an issue in this case. His murder, however," Miller went on as voices again rose in objection, "will be avenged in good time." Turning his attention fully back to Daniel, Miller continued, "Given the circumstances of your heroic deeds, I was prepared to lighten your sentence to five hours in the pillory, and have done with it," the judge said, glaring sternly at Daniel. "But now we discover you are also an adulterer, and that we cannot abide."

Adulterer. The ugly word brought up the taste of bile in Mary's throat. She heard soft weeping, and imagined Rebecca dabbing at her teary eyes while the crease between Lydia's brows deepened.

"And so," concluded Miller, "we sentence you to receive forty lashes on the naked back and banished from Hereford." The crowd murmured and Judge Miller raised his voice to be heard over the rumble. "You will return with your lawful wife to your home, never to set foot in Hereford again."

Behind her, Mary heard a woman mutter scornfully, and assumed it was Lydia. "If you have nothing to say for yourself," Judge Miller went on, "We'll proceed to the next case."

"The devil take you," Daniel said, his defiance resounding clearly. The congregation gasped as thunder rumbled gently. Mary's mouth fell open. He glared brazenly at Miller, his hands clenched into angry fists. His eyes glinted stonily and before the judge could react, Daniel spit. The crowd murmured in shock as the spittle hit the lectern and trickled down. It slid past the great Eye of God like a tear, leaving a wet trail.

Clearly enraged, Judge Miller's face darkened. "Remove this man from my presence and secure him to the whipping post! He'll receive his forty lashes immediately following the sentencing of Mary Case."

Mary clamped both hands over her mouth as her empty stomach threatened to heave. Constable Hart's brooding eyes met hers for a moment before he nodded at James, who grasped Daniel by the arm and turned him about to leave. Even then, Daniel wouldn't meet her eyes. A heart-broken wail pierced the air as Rebecca Eames sobbed, "Son!" Mary's feelings for Daniel had cooled, but his mother's cries brought her to tears and she turned behind her to search for the older woman. Lydia met Mary's eyes with an icy stare while Rebecca had turned in her seat to watch Daniel be escorted out. As he passed the seated onlookers and disappeared out the door, Rebecca turned to the front again, her green eyes swimming in tears. Her apron obscured her nose and mouth as her gnarled hands pressed the linen garment against her face. Rebecca's eyes locked with Mary's, and Mary felt a sob rip from her own throat. *Forgive me for bringing such misery upon you, Widow Eames!* Mary wanted to cry, suddenly feeling that she alone was the cause of all this misfortune.

The gavel rapped firmly and Judge Miller demanded order. "Mary Case," he said sternly. "You may approach."

Mary broke eye contact with Rebecca reluctantly and turned to face the front. Goodwives Ellis and Hawkins each gripped an elbow, but Mary shook them off. She stood on trembling legs and approached the judge and magistrates. Hart remained in his spot, regarding her dolefully. The magistrates glowered at her with disdain, and she could barely hear Judge Miller's words over the ringing in her ears.

"Mary Case, you are charged with fornication and with the murder of Thomas Dirby while aiding in the escape of Daniel Eames. This is a capital offense, and so we hereby sentence you to hang by the neck until dead."

The words failed to register, and Mary swayed on her feet as the room reacted. She thought she heard her father cry out, and then from the woman's side, a raspy voice protested, "Your Honor, she can't be hanged!"

The onlookers grew more excited, and Miller again rapped the gavel multiple times. Mary glanced over her shoulder and saw Widow Eames standing, both hands planted on firmly on her cane.

"Silence!" Miller demanded. "And who defies our ruling?"

"I do," Daniel's mother said. "This young maid can't be hanged because she is with child!"

The meetinghouse burst into an uproar just as a loud peal of thunder resounded overhead. It took several moments before order was restored, and Mary felt the floor roll beneath her feet.

"She's going to faint!" Someone cried just as she felt her knees give way. Lightning illuminated the room just before she lost consciousness and collapsed into Absalom Hart's arms.

Chapter Twenty-eight

Mary awoke to find herself perched on a stool, placed squarely in front of the scowling Judge Miller and his magistrates. The pounding of Miller's gavel made her head throb, and she swayed dizzily. She sensed someone standing behind her, and felt steadying hands on her shoulders. She recognized the hands as those of Goody Ellis. To her right, Absalom Hart stood like a mighty oak against a violent wind. She closed her eyes against a wave of nausea and willed her stomach to settle.

"This new information puts Mary Case's fate into a new light," Miller's voice sounded far away. "Since a woman in her condition cannot be hanged, we will postpone her sentence until the child is born. After such time, she will be dispatched accordingly. However, for the time being, she will be fined six pounds."

Mary opened her eyes and blinked in stunned confusion. *So my life is spared, for the time being,* she thought, placing her hands on her abdomen. *Spared because of this child.* Then the fog in her mind began to thin and matter of the fine emerged. *Where will I get six pounds to pay that?*

"Your honor, if I may--" Hart began.

Miller shot Hart a hostile look. "Constable, this case is about to adjourn."

Hart cleared his throat. "I beg that the murder charges be dropped."

The crowd murmured curiously.

"On what grounds?"

"On the grounds that her only accuser was Noah Parker, and he cannot testify. Jailer Dirby's heart could likely have given out, or the poor sot could have passed in a drunken stupor. There's no proof Mary Case had anything to do with his death."

His words were punctuated by another rumble of thunder, and the crowd murmured excitedly as Mary looked up at Hart gratefully. His eyes were fixed on Judge Miller, his jaw set firmly. Mary turned to Miller, who was deliberating with his fellow magistrates. After a moment, a decision was reached, and he glowered from the pulpit like a hawk whose prey had eluded him.

"We agree that there is no existing evidence, nor is there a witness, to bind Mary Case to the death of Jailer Dirby. But the fine of six pounds still stands." The gavel thumped once. "This court is adjourned."

Mary gulped, her shoulders sagging in relief. Next to her, Hart exhaled through his mouth, clearly relieved himself. She heard the crowd muttering and stirring behind her. She felt as if she'd taken root and couldn't rise from the stool. As the magistrates rose and exited the meetinghouse from a side door, her father came forward. He took her hands in his and gently pulled her to her feet. Her face flared with shame as he lifted her chin with a finger. A myriad of emotions—grief, love, relief—played on his features, and Mary crumpled against his thin chest.

"I'm sorry, Father," she wept. "I'm sorry for shaming you. I'm sorry for Lizzie, and for--"

He hushed her, rocking her slowly in his arms. Mary couldn't remember the last time he'd held her...had he even once, since Mother died? She breathed in his scent while her tears soaked into his doublet. "You've nothing to beg forgiveness for, Daughter."

"But...where will we get the six pounds? And I'm...I'm carrying Daniel's bastard child...."

"The fine will get paid," Richard assured her softly. He said nothing of the child, and Mary wondered if he truly did forgive her. He pulled her away from his chest and peered sadly at her as she wiped her eyes and nose with her apron. She glanced around the room and discovered only Daniel's family remained. Apparently Goodwives

Ellis and Hawkins felt their services were no longer needed, and had abandoned her. Rebecca Eames looked heartbroken, her son John's arm draped protectively over her shaking shoulders. Only Lydia Eames remained stoic, her granite face unreadable. *How can you be so cold?* Mary wanted to ask her. *Surely you have some feelings in all this!* She averted her eyes from Lydia's and shuddered.

Behind Richard stood Absalom Hart, his brooding face full of concern. He shifted awkwardly from one foot to the other and was about to speak when James burst into the meetinghouse, rain water pouring from the brim of his felt hat. Mary heard Riff, still evidently tied to the whipping post, bark in alarm. Hoof beats competed with the thunder as the storm raged on past the open meetinghouse door.

"Come quick, sir! The militia's back!" James cried. "With them two men from Salem!"

All eyes looked to Hart, who stepped forward. "Where's Eames?"

"I thought it best to secure him in the cell when I saw that mob coming," James replied.

"Good man," Hart said. To the small group that clustered near him, he said, "Stay inside."

"Allow me to help, Constable," John Eames said, releasing his mother's shoulders. "He is my brother, after all."

The two men shared a meaningful glance before Hart nodded his consent. "Muskets are useless in this rain. Have you a knife?"

"Aye."

Constable Hart turned to Richard. "Reverend, will you stay with the women?"

Richard nodded. "My hands are too unsteady for combat."

Hart snatched his hat from the pew it rested on and slapped it on his head. "Bolt the door behind us then, Reverend."

As Hart marched towards the door followed by his deputy and John Eames, Mary's eyes sought Rebecca. The little woman leaned on her cane, looking after the departing men with a trembling chin. Lydia Eames stood nearby, her arms crossed tightly against her chest. *Can you at least comfort your mother-in-law?* Mary wanted to scream. Instead, she traversed the floor in three wide steps and embraced

Daniel's mother. Rebecca Eames felt thin and slight in her arms, and she dared not hug her too tight lest she break any fragile bones.

"Please forgive me for the shame and pain I've brought upon you, Widow Eames!" she blubbered into the woman's bony shoulder.

She felt an arm go around her, and both women remained locked in the embrace for several moments. Rebecca smelled faintly of wood smoke and moldy hay, and Mary found a measure of comfort in the woman's scent as she inhaled.

"Hush," Rebecca whispered soothingly. "You've naught to be forgiven for." When Mary pulled away, Rebecca's sad eyes glimmered with fresh tears. "You carry my grandchild, which I see as a blessing."

Mary saw Lydia's jaw drop open. "*Mother Eames!*" she cried indignantly. "How can you call her bastard your *grandchild* with such welcome?"

Rebecca's green eyes darted to Lydia. "Again, I insist you apologize for your rudeness, Daughter."

"I won't!" Lydia declared, her shrill voice echoing off the walls. "I'm the wronged party here! She should apologize to *me!*"

Mary slowly withdrew from Rebecca's embrace as an unexpected rage bubbled within her. Her body stiffened as she turned to face Daniel's wife. This time she met the woman's hateful glare with equal animosity.

"I don't expect an apology from you, Goodwife Eames," she said evenly. "Methinks your outrage is misdirected. I knew not Daniel was married, and any contempt you feel would be better directed at him." She squared her shoulders and continued haughtily, "However, the more I bear witness to your disposition, the less I blame him for abandoning you!"

Lydia gaped in indignation and raised an arm as if to slap Mary, but Richard stepped between them and intervened.

"Daughter! Goodwife Eames!" Richard said, trying to maintain peace within the meetinghouse walls. "This is unseemly behavior. Pray, seat yourselves until the constable comes for us, and let's all pray for deliverance through this difficult time."

Lydia continued to glower at Mary and then at Richard before seating herself with a graceless *plop* on the nearest pew, her arms crossed and her scowl ever deeper. Mary looked from Lydia to Rebecca, then helped the older woman to a pew, the cane tapping lightly on the floor with each small step.

Richard remained alone near the pulpit, wringing his trembling hands anxiously. Rebecca placed a hand in Mary's before she bowed her head. Mary grasped the older woman's hand gently as Richard began, "Heavenly Father, we ask for Your merciful forgiveness--"

I'm afraid I could not keep my mind on Father's prayer. Instead, I kept my eyes open, trying to memorize every feature of your grandmother's hand as it lay in mine. I traced the blue veins that rose like worms beneath the thin skin. The swollen joints, as knobby and gnarled as old tree trunks, bespoke of endless hours of labor. I gently turned the palm up and examined its intricate web of lines. Those hands had loved and nurtured, toiled and lost. They'd survived horrors I could barely imagine, and yet they were warm and loving. I was thus entranced, thinking of all this woman had endured, when a solemn "Amen" roused me from my musings.

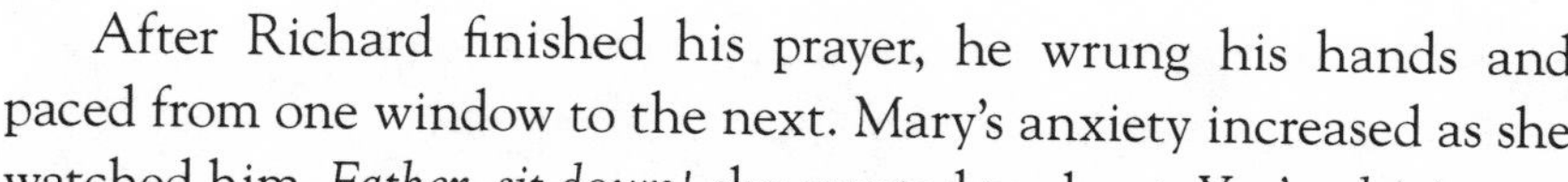

After Richard finished his prayer, he wrung his hands and paced from one window to the next. Mary's anxiety increased as she watched him. *Father, sit down!* she wanted to shout. *You're driving me to distraction!*

"—entirely too thin," Rebecca Eames was saying.

"Beg pardon?"

Mary glanced at the older woman, whose green eyes scrutinized her with motherly concern. "You're skin and bones. 'Twill make for a sickly babe if you don't eat more."

Mary smiled at Rebecca's solicitude. "I've had no appetite for some time."

Rebecca nodded knowingly. "'Twas the same with me when I was carrying Daniel."

At the mention of her son's name, Rebecca's eyes softened and grew red around the rims. She appeared to be recalling an earlier time, perhaps when Daniel was a precocious youngster or an innocent babe. Mary gently squeezed Rebecca's hand and said, "I'm sorry to have brought such heartache to you and your family."

The crooked fingers returned her squeeze as a tear rolled down Rebecca's pock marked cheek. "Although we mayn't understand why, everything happens as the Lord intends it to. You and my son were meant to meet, and produce this child."

Mary's eyes smarted with hot tears as she whispered anxiously, "I fear for this child's future."

Rebecca regarded her with knowing silence. "'Twill be a test of your faith, but that's the purpose of faith. To see us through difficult times."

Mary gaped in awe. "How, after all you've endured, can you retain such a steadfast faith? Daniel told me of the abuse you suffered in the Salem jail, and I can't even begin to fathom --"

The older woman smiled sadly. "The horror of it still lives in me, but even greater is the loss of my beloved husband. The Lord took him two months ago, just afore Daniel left us. Yet, I remain, and so I must have a purpose unfulfilled." Rebecca withdrew her hand from Mary's and patted the young woman's knee. "Mayhap my purpose is to remind you to embrace your faith."

Mary's heart warmed and expanded like a mound of bread dough rising in a temperate room. "Despite the circumstances that caused it, I'm glad to have met you, Widow Eames."

Rebecca gave her a bemused look. "I'm but a poor widow, nothing more."

Oh, but you're so much more! Mary wanted to argue. She couldn't name the quality that the older woman possessed, but it left Mary in awe. Was it grace? Fortitude? Compassion? If the stories Daniel had told her were true, Widow Eames survived a stay in hell and back, keeping her faith and benevolence intact.

"The storm appears to be letting up," Richard said, twisting a handkerchief as he peered out a rain-splashed window.

Lightning again lit up the sky, followed by another *Boom* that rattled the meetinghouse windows. Mary looked up from her lap, ears ringing from the report. She looked at her father, who stopped pacing before the altar. He appeared stricken.

"Accursed thunder," Mary heard Lydia mutter.

"That wasn't a thunderclap," Richard said, his words edgy with trepidation. "I fear that was a musket shot."

Chapter Twenty-Nine

"Reverend Case, open the door!"

Constable Hart's words were muffled as they penetrated the heavy door. Mary and the other women rose as Richard approached the barred door with an anxious face.

"Have a care, Father!" Mary cried, reaching for him as he passed by her.

"Constable Hart wouldn't bid us open were it not safe," Richard said to the women before he slid back the bolt.

Mary and Rebecca clutched each other as they inched towards the door. Mary didn't look back to see if Daniel's wife had joined them and imagined the scornful woman still sat with her arms folded against her bosom and the lines of her sour face deepening. But then she heard another set of foot falls behind her, and realized Lydia Eames was trailing behind them after all. She forced the thought of the scorned woman out of her mind and concentrated on taking small, slow steps to accommodate Rebecca.

Richard unlatched and opened the door, finding Absalom Hart accompanied by John Eames. They supported a bloodied young James, whose hatless head drooped forward. The men were drenched in rainwater, and Mary stifled a shiver as she looked at them. A burst of rain-scoured air wafted in with them and Mary caught a glimpse of the crowd outside, yelling and gesticulating, before Richard hastily closed and latched it again.

"James caught a musket in his shoulder," Hart explained as he and

John dragged the injured man to a pew. "Soon as the rain let up, some fool let off a shot; it's incited them all to riot."

The three women hastened to examine the wound, and Mary took fleeting notice that Lydia seemed animated by the emergency. "Is there a bucket of water and linens I could use for bandages?" she asked, directing her words at Richard.

"Aye," he replied. "I'll fetch them."

James' head lolled feebly as Mary and Rebecca removed his ruined shirt and pressed it to the wound. The metallic scent of blood induced more queasiness, and Mary clamped her jaw against the compulsion to vomit. Richard returned with a bucket of tepid water and Lydia pushed Mary aside, her scowling face hard and determined. Mary found herself admiring Lydia's compassion. *She does have a heart after all*, she thought, watching the linen beneath Lydia's hands blush red with blood before it was replaced with a fresh cloth.

"The mob out there is anxious for the whipping to commence," Constable Hart said. "Mary, will you stay and tend to James?"

Before Mary could respond, Lydia Eames looked up from her patient. "I'll stay." She gave Rebecca a meaningful look. "I'd rather tend to this youngster than lay eyes on Daniel ever again, Mother Eames. Forgive me, but that's how I feel."

Lydia's disregard for Daniel seemed to surprise everyone but Rebecca, who merely nodded. "It appears you've said your last to each other."

"Take my arm, Mother," John said. "The steps are slick from the rain."

Hart looked up from his pale deputy and raised a hand. "John, I thought I might impose upon you to help me fetch your brother from the jail."

The two men regarded each other somberly until Rebecca said, "Very well. Mary will escort me."

Mary met the older woman's gaze with surprise. As Rebecca slipped her free arm through hers, Mary was again struck by the woman's grace. She patted Rebecca's hand gently as Hart opened the door.

The rain-scoured air brought the courtyard into sharp focus.

Guiding Daniel's mother carefully down the slick steps, Mary squinted against the bright sunlight. Past Hart's and John's backs stood the assembled crowd. They resembled a hungry pack of wolves, anxious for the kill. Judge Miller stood with the other magistrates, rain still dripping from the brim of this black hat. He strummed his fingers restlessly against the small Bible he clasped to his chest. Riff remained tied to the whipping post. When he saw them approach, he got off his haunches and whined. Corwin stood with a wooden pike in his right hand and bloodstained bag he grasped in his left. Next to him stood Dounton, leering at Mary through a cloud of pipe smoke. When his snakelike eyes met hers, Mary shivered with disgust.

"There stands the Devil's henchman," she heard Rebecca murmur. "If not Satan himself."

Mary wasn't sure if Rebecca was referring to Corwin, Dounton, or both, but she

agreed silently with Rebecca's assessment. She helped Rebecca negotiate the bottom steps of the meetinghouse. Their footfalls splashed softly in the rain-soaked grass and she felt the hem of her skirt dampen. She and Rebecca stationed themselves across from the main crowd as Hart and John marched somberly across the courtyard to retrieve Daniel. Richard stood beside them, his hands quivering like aspen leaves. *Poor Father,* she thought, suddenly realizing she'd never considered how the loss of his wife and daughter affected him. He seemed to have aged twenty years in the past three months, and she was going to offer him her hand when Riff let out an anguished bark. Mary followed Riff's eyes and saw the three men heading towards the whipping post. She gasped—or was it Rebecca who gasped?—when she saw Daniel. His hands were bound at the wrists and his buckskin tunic had been removed. A good week's growth of beard sprung from his lower face and his green eyes glinted in defiance beneath the brim of his felt hat. His back bore a network of welts from past whippings, and Mary remembered tracing them lightly with her fingertips when they coupled. Hart tucked a coiled bullwhip beneath his left arm while he untied Daniel's wrists. Riff barked again, wagging his tail in anticipation of being reunited with his master.

"Someone remove that beast," Judge Miller ordered as Daniel and his escorts approached. John left his brother's side and knelt on one knee to untie the dog. As he worked the knots loose, Mary felt Rebecca release her arm and take several steps towards Daniel.

"Your honor," she said in her rasping voice, "might you allow a mother a final word with her son?"

"Get back in the crowd, you old wretch!" Dounton snarled, giving Rebecca a shove. With only her cane for support, she tottered and fell with a *splash* into a puddle. The crowd gasped in unison and Mary shrieked, "No!" before running to assist the fallen woman. She and John reached Rebecca at the same moment, but John was preoccupied with restraining Riff, and Mary alone helped Rebecca to her feet.

"I told you in Salem," Daniel raged, lunging at Dounton. "If you ever touch my mother again, I'll strangle you with my bare hands!"

The two men rolled in the mud, hands on each other's throats. Somewhere in the scuffle Dounton lost his pipe. Riff strained at the leash, barking and snarling while John held him back. The crowd encouraged the brawl enthusiastically while Judge Miller demanded someone separate the two. Hart stepped forward immediately, dropping the whip in the mud before pulling Daniel off Dounton.

"Eames!" Mary heard Hart yell as she helped the fallen woman to her feet. "You'll only make things worse for yourself. Let up!"

Both combatants were covered in mud, and Daniel's eyes blazed with fury as he shook Hart's hand off his arm. The crowd seemed to hold their collective breath as Daniel addressed Dounton, who remained on his hands and knees in the mud, searching for something.

"I'll kill you, Dounton!" Daniel growled. "If I have to return from the fires of Hell to do it!"

"Enough!" Judge Miller bellowed. "Let's proceed with the punishment."

Dounton found the stem of his pipe, but it was missing the bowl. He threw it aside and bared his teeth like a mad dog. "I should flog you ten more times for the pipe you broke!" He scrambled to his feet and grabbed Daniel, dragging him to the whipping post. When Daniel's arms were secured around the post and his bare back was displayed before the crowd, all eyes rested on Absalom Hart, who'd retrieved the bullwhip from the mud.

"Constable," Judge Miller intoned. "Commence, if you will."

Mary held her breath as she and Rebecca watched Hart. The constable looked at the whip in his hands, then at Daniel, who returned Hart's gaze coldly.

"Get on with it, Hart," Daniel said flatly.

Hart regarded Daniel silently, but before he could perform his duty, Dounton stepped up and snatched the whip from Hart's hands.

"I'll show you how justice is doled out in Salem," he said, unfurling the whip with a loud crack that made Mary wince.

Hart regarded Dounton steadily. "Forty lashes, Dounton. No more. If you hurt this man more than that, I'll throw you in the stocks for a week."

Dounton wiped mud from his face and spat on the ground. He dismissed Hart with a sneer as Corwin thrust the pike into the earth directly in Daniel's view. "Eames, I brought a friend of yours to witness your scourging."

Mary glanced at the pike with dread as Corwin withdrew something from the bloody sack. She knew what it was before he jammed it on the pike's tip. The crowd again gasped and Mary clamped her jaw firmly against the bile that rose in her throat.

Impaled on the pike was Charles' severed head.

Not Charles! His glassy eyes stared into nothingness as she remembered the strong, confident warrior who had been so gentle with his children. *Daniel was right,* she thought dismally. *'Tis we who are the savages.*

As Mary looked on in horror, Judge Miller regarded the gruesome display with a look of disgust, his face blanching slightly.

"Proceed!"

John, still wrangling a distraught Riff, stepped beside his mother. "Don't watch, Mother," he advised quietly, shielding her with his arm. "And stop up your ears."

Mary embraced Rebecca's shoulders while John obscured her view. The first crack of the whip made Mary jump. Beneath her arms,

Rebecca sobbed, and Mary soon joined her. Mary wanted to cover her own ears, but that would mean releasing her grip on Rebecca, who likely would collapse if Mary didn't support her. Riff pressed against her skirts and emitted a mournful howl.

The whippings continued and the crowd was silent except for a few women weeping. *Thirty-seven, thirty-eight, thirty-nine....* Mary couldn't help counting them off in her head. She closed her eyes tightly and buried her face against the hood of Rebecca's woolen cloak. She breathed in the woman's scent and detected the smell of heartbreaking despair.

Seared into my memory for all time is the image of your father slumped against that horrid post. The ropes binding his wrists were all that kept him from falling into the bloody puddle of mud. Your grandmother approached her son, and the dear woman begged him to come home to Boxford. I couldn't believe he hadn't succumbed to the pain, his head hanging limply off his bloody shoulders. I strained to hear his response to her pleas, but his words were for her ears only. Whatever he said brought upon his mother's face a look of pure sorrow. I remember how deathly silent the crowd was as she gently wiped his face with her apron before putting a hand on his cheek and kissing his forehead as mothers do. Then she straightened her posture as well as her stooping shoulders would allow, her red-rimmed eyes glimmering with tears, as she hobbled unassisted to her former spot next to John and I. There were no words for that solemn, heart-breaking moment, and all I could do was drape my arm over her trembling shoulders whilst Riff, that faithful beast, let out a sorrowful howl.

Chapter Thirty

September, 1712
Hereford, CT

Mary found Kezia where she left her, still perched on the large grey rock. The young woman's cheeks were tear-streaked and her green eyes rimmed with red when Mary approached her.

"Oh, Mother," she breathed, dabbing at her eyes with her apron. "After reading those missives, I've so many questions."

Mary smiled softly and approached her daughter. She was relieved Kezia wasn't angry or hateful. "Then ask, my darling girl."

"What happened after…after the whipping?"

Mary set the sewing basket on the rock and seated herself next to Kezia. Her hands gripped the handle so tightly her knuckles turned white. "I've tried to forget most of that dark day, but I can tell you your grandmother, Uncle John, and…Lydia made haste to return to their home in Boxford. It being September, it was a busy time for farmers, and John needed to get back to work. I had barely time to give that dear woman a last embrace before she and her kin departed—of their own means, mind you. They refused to be brought back to Massachusetts with Corwin and Dounton, quite understandably." The mention of their names left a nasty taste in Mary's mouth and she grimaced as their faces materialized in her memory. "I was fortunate to never see them again, although I did hear Corwin died of a heart attack just two years later. And the other--"

Dounton. She didn't know whom she despised more, him or Corwin. "Your Uncle John penned me a letter that he heard some time after returning to Salem, that hateful creature choked to death on a tough piece of beef." Mary resisted the urge to grin as she added, "I sometimes think it was Daniel making good his word to strangle that dark-hearted man."

"And what of my…my grandmother?" Kezia pressed.

"She lives still, in Boxford. She was but recently pardoned, and her good name has been restored. Your Uncle John again kept me abreast of the situation."

Kezia dropped her eyes to the papers on the table. "Mayhap we could visit her one day."

Mary smiled. The thought of seeing Widow Eames again would warm her soul, but she doubted at the likelihood of it.

"What happened to—to my father, after he was banished from Hereford?"

She took a deep breath and said, "When you were in your second year, Constable Hart returned from hunting and knocked on the rectory door. He begged to speak with me privately and told me he'd come upon the remains of a man in the woods."

Kezia's breath caught in her throat as she listened, her mouth slightly agape.

"Animals had gotten to it, but there was still a mass of red hair on the head," Mary went on, shivering at the memory. Her fingers released the handle and burrowed beneath the sewing notions until they withdrew a bundle carefully wrapped in homespun. Mary placed it reverently in her lap and unwrapped it to expose a beaded belt coiled within. She unfurled it gently, inhaling the scent of old leather as she did so. "Next to it, as if protecting it even in death, was the carcass of a black, shaggy dog with this very belt around its neck. The good Constable knew for certain then he'd found your father and Riff, and he sent out a team to retrieve the sad find. The magistrates wouldn't allow the banished man's bones to rest in Hereford's cemetery, so again Absalom took it upon himself to dig a grave for them both on his own property."

Realization settled over Kezia's pretty face and she whispered, "Here?"

Mary handed Kezia the belt. "Aye. Right alongside this rock." She smiled sadly. "'Tis part of why I spend so much time here…to be near your father and that devoted dog of his."

Kezia folded the letters and set them in her lap before accepting the belt. Her long fingers glided over the smooth beads tenderly. She pressed the beads to her lips and kissed them, bringing a painful lump to Mary's throat. My *dear girl,* she thought. *I wish 'twere a happier tale.* When she could speak, her voice was tight. "After Father died, I came into my inheritance with no one to contest it. I was finally able to pay my own fine, and put all that behind me. Then I married your stepfather, and here we are."

Kezia smiled, and wiped a tear from her cheek. "Father has always been so good to me."

Mary nodded. "He's a blessing of a man," Mary agreed.

"Thank you for allowing me to read these, Mother. So many questions have tormented me my whole life. Now I have the answers, sad as they are."

Mary sank her front teeth into her bottom lip, relieved Kezia held no resentment towards her. She smiled and was about to speak when Kezia rose from the rock and pointed. "Here comes Father!"

Mary turned to see her husband approaching. His sullen face lit up at the sight of them, and Mary's heart swelled as her daughter ran to greet him, planting a kiss on his cheek.

They adore each other, Mary thought, her heart swelling with love as they drew near, holding hands. She got to her feet as her husband removed his hat. His eyes traveled from the folded parchments to the beaded belt that rested on the rock.

"Good day, Wife," he said, his eyes finally settling on Mary. "So the girl knows, and all is well?"

"Aye, Husband," she replied, reaching for both his and Kezia's hand. They formed an unbreakable triangle beneath the shade of the poplars, and Mary never felt more blessed. "Welcome home, Absalom."

Author's Notes

This book immediately follows the events at the end of *Puritan Witch: The Redemption of Rebecca Eames*. Although this book is fiction, it does contain a few historical facts:

Daniel Eames later had a daughter, Kezia, with Mary Case. The child was baptised on 1 Mar 1695/6 in Hartford, CT.

> "Mary Case of Hartford complayned of Daniel Eames late of boxford for begetting her with child whoe being examined the sayd Eames & Mary Case both in court acknowledged that they had committed folly together sometime in January last by which the sayd Mary Case is with child as she sayth & that sayd Daniels wickedness is aggravated in that he had a wife of his owne at that time he committed that folly. We seize & sentence him the sayd Daniel Eames to be severly whipt upon the naked body on Wednesday imediately after the lecture And the sayd Mary Case for her committing fornication with the sayd Eames whoe is a marryoud person & his wife now Liveing we doe sentence her to pay a fine of six punds or be severly whipt on the naked body as soon as she shall be in a capacity to receive her punishment & we doe order the sayd Eames to depart the colony forthwith & to return to his wife and famaly as the law requires." "Session of

the hartford County Court, 18 June 1695, Lt Col John Allyn, Mr Nath, Stanly and Capt Jacob Stanly, presiding." Vol. 5, p. 87 1 4

This is the only information I could find on Daniel Eames after his involvement with the Salem Witch trials. I changed the town's name to Hereford and populated it with fictional characters. Mary Case's parents' names were Richard and Elizabeth Purchas, but I don't know anything more about her family.

William Dounton was the jailer in Salem during the witch trials, and George Corwin, High Sheriff of Essex County, Massachusetts, died of a heart attack April 12, 1696.

The names for the Algonquin Indian characters were obtained by a list of Native American baby names at www.cutebabynames.com . Other information on the Native Americans was obtained by various book and online sources.

Daniel Eames was my eighth uncle.

Glossary

Bann Proclamation of marriage

Baseborn Illegitimate

Below the Salt In Colonial households, the father sat at the head of the table, his wife and older children seated at the same end. The salt cellar was placed in the middle of the table, marking the head and foot. Younger children or those of lesser status sat at the lower end of the table, or "below the salt."

Bonded Out In colonial days, older children were often bonded out to other families as indentured servants.

Footpad A thief, like a highwayman, but unlike a highwayman, a footpad travels without a horse.

Mettle Courage

Physick a medicine

Samp a common porridge dish frequently eaten in Colonial days.

Stoups jugs

Tithingman a church officer

Winding Sheets Linens used to shroud a dead body